7-9-75

WHERE THERE'S SMOKE

Random House New York

Ed McBain

WHERE THERE'S SMOKE

THIS IS FOR MY SON,
RICHARD HUNTER—
WHO SUGGESTED THE CHARACTER

The city in these pages is imaginary.
The people, the places are all fictitious.
As vaporous as smoke.

WHERE THERE'S SMOKE

MY NAME is Benjamin Smoke.

Spare me, please, the tired queries and pointless witticisms. I'm proudly descended from a long line of Dutch burghers, one of whom, three generations back, arrived in this country bearing the name Evert Johannes van der Smoak. A petty immigration official promptly changed my grandfather's name and recorded it for posterity as Everett Smoke. This was common practice during the early part of the century, when the American melting pot reduced to common residue European names that had survived for generations. There was neither malice nor grand design in this simplification of names too difficult to spell or pronounce; there was merely expediency, and perhaps foresight. A great deal of paperwork was involved in the naturalization process, you see. Errors both present and future could easily be avoided by taking a person named Sygmunt Laskiewicz and renaming him Sig Lasky at the port of entry. You might argue that the process was dehumanizing. On the other hand, it was small enough price to pay for admission to this great land of opportunity.

I'm a retired police lieutenant.

I used to command an eighteen-man squad of detectives in one of this city's busier precincts. I quit because I got bored. Without attempting to sound immodest (I'm normally shy and self-effacing), there's really very little challenge to police work. Once you get the knack of it, it becomes easy. And boring. You most certainly get the knack of it after twenty-four years on the force—as Patrolman, Detective Third, Detective Second, Detective First, and finally, Detective-Lieutenant in charge of a squad. Burglaries, muggings, robberies, rapes; forgeries, frauds, arsons, and common misdemeanors; murders by ax, dagger, switchblade, shotgun, rope, ice pick, poison, pistol, shovel, hammer, hatchet, baseball bat, or fists; crimes of commission or omission—*all* lose whatever sense of poetry or glamor they may have once possessed. Tedium. It all reduces itself to tedium in triplicate.

I'm forty-eight years old.

I'm six feet three inches tall, and I weigh an even two hundred pounds. (My weight hasn't varied since I was twenty. Not an ounce. I make sure it doesn't.) I have green eyes and hair I prefer to think of as iron-gray, worn short but not close-cropped, parted on the left-hand side. There's a knife scar on my right cheek, memento of a scuffle I had with a cheap thief three days after I'd been promoted to Detective Third. To complete the B-sheet, I have a tattoo on the biceps of my left arm, "Peg" in a blood-red heart, blue dagger piercing it, a permanent reminder of a foolish love affair I had while serving with the United States Navy in San Francisco during World War II. Peg was a prostitute, I later learned.

Since my retirement, I've privately investigated only four cases. I do not have a private investigator's license, and I never expect to apply for one. Whatever anyone may tell you about licensed private eyes, they're hired mostly to find missing persons or to get the goods on adulterous husbands; my aspirations are higher. I have a Carry permit for a .38 Detective's Special, but I've never had to use the gun since I left the force, and I rarely bother clipping it to my belt. I also own a gold lieutenant's shield which I carry in a small leather case. It was a personal retirement gift from the Chief of Detectives, and it has served me well over the past three years. I would rather part with my pistol and my shoes than that magic little shield. I live fairly comfortably on my pension and on the dividends from some stocks I inherited when my father died. I suppose I might be considered a happy man.

In fact, I have only one regret.

I've never investigated a case I couldn't solve. I've never encountered the perfect crime.

1

I WENT to see Abner Boone only because his urgent phone call seemed to promise something mildly interesting. I arrived at his place of business on Hennessy Street at nine o'clock on a Monday morning in September. Abner was an undertaker dressed in his customary weeds—black suit, black shoes and socks, black tie, white shirt. He led me through the front of his cheerful establishment, past two viewing rooms and a chapel, and then opened a door that led to a room in which a pair of closed coffins rested on sawhorses. Two windows with drawn shades were on one wall of the room. On the other wall, there was a door that had obviously been forced open with a crowbar; there were fresh scars and jagged splinters on the wooden jamb. No professional, this thief.

"I'm glad you could come, Lieutenant," Abner said. "If word of this—"

"Abner," I said, "excuse me, but I'm no longer a lieutenant."

"But you still investigate crimes," he said.

"Hardly ever," I said.

"Lieutenant," he said, "this is a crime of great enormity."

"Have you contacted the police yet?"

"Of course not."

"Why not?"

"Lieutenant," he said, "I couldn't take that chance. Suppose a newspaper reporter got wind of this? I'd be the laughingstock of the profession. I called you immediately."

"You woke me up," I said.

"I'm sorry about that," he said.

"All right, tell me what happened."

"Someone has stolen a corpse," Abner said.

"I know that. When?"

"Last night sometime."

"Where was the corpse the last time you saw it?"

"In the casket behind you."

"Male or female?"

"Male."

"Clothed or naked?"

"Fully clothed."

"Wearing what?"

"Blue pin-striped suit, white shirt, dark-blue necktie, blue socks, black shoes."

"Embalmed?"

"Yes, of course. I always do that at once. Certainly within the first two hours."

"When was the body delivered to you?"

"At eight o'clock last night. It came directly from the hospital. Saint Augustine's, on Third and Sussex."

"How'd the man die?"

"In an automobile accident on the Harbor Highway. He broke his neck on impact when his car crashed into a concrete pillar."

"Give me his name."

"Anthony Gibson."

"Age?"

"Forty-two."

"Height?"

"Five feet eleven, I would say."

"Weight?"

"A hundred eighty-five, more or less."

"Color of hair?"

"Brown."

"Eyes?"

"Brown."

"Any identifying marks, scars, tattoos?"

"None."

"Except for your embalming incisions, you mean."

"Yes."

Over the course of twenty-four years on the force, I'd had ample opportunity to observe a great many corpses, those recently deceased as well as those exhumed for autopsy. Most of the exhumed bodies had already been embalmed, of course, and it doesn't take much time to learn exactly where a mortician makes his incisions. To draw out the contents of the stomach, intestines, and bladder (forgive me, ma'am, but police work sometimes entailed a bit more than typing up a burglary report), the embalmer normally makes a small puncture in the upper middle region of the abdomen and then inserts a large hollow needle attached to a suction apparatus. This trocar, as it's called, is also used to drain the body of its blood, the embalmer's incisions for this purpose being made over large blood vessels in the neck, the groin, and the armpit. Embalming fluid—a solution of formaldehyde that causes coagulation of protein—is then injected by trocar or tube into the vascular system and the body cavities. On the off chance that Abner might have used a different technique (we all have our idiosyncrasies), I asked him exactly where he'd made his incisions.

"Neck, groin, armpit, epigastrium," he said.

"Who contacted you regarding funeral arrangements?"

"His wife. Rhoda Gibson. She called me from the hospital at about seven."

"And did she come here when the body was delivered?"

"Yes. She and her son."

"What's *his* name?"

"Jeffrey Gibson. Big fellow with a red beard, maybe twenty-one, twenty-two years old."

"Where do they live?"

"1214 Matthews Avenue."

"And you say the body was delivered at eight last night?"

"Yes."

"And you embalmed it immediately."

"Well, as soon as the family left."

"What time did *you* leave here?"

"At about midnight."

"And what time did you open the place this morning?"

"I was here at seven-thirty. I called you the moment I discovered the theft. Will you help me, Lieutenant?"

"Maybe," I said. "Any jewelry on the corpse? Rings, watch, identification bracelet?"

"Nothing."

"All right, Abner, do you have any personal enemies or business rivals?"

"None who would do something like this."

"Are you fooling around with anyone's wife, mother, sister, or cousin?"

"I'm a happily married man."

"Have you received any threatening telephone calls or letters?"

"Never."

"Can you think of anyone who might want to cause you professional embarrassment?"

"Not a soul."

"Have you had any recent arguments or disputes with families for whom you've made funeral arrangements?"

"None."

"Have you been dunning anyone for non-payment of bills?"

"No."

"What about your employees? Do you get along with them?"

"I work alone, except for my drivers. This is a very small operation."

"Any of your drivers ask for a raise recently?"

"No. Lieutenant, why would anyone want to steal a dead body?"

"I don't know."

"Is there no longer any respect for the dead?"

"There never was, Abner. Anything else stolen? Besides the body?"

"Nothing. Will you help me?"

"Yes," I said.

Maybe I was rising to the bait too quickly.

The Penal Law in this state is specific about the theft of dead bodies. The pertinent section is appropriately if unimaginatively titled *Body Stealing*, and it reads:

> *Sec. 2216. A person who removes the dead body of a human being, or any part thereof from a grave, vault, or other place where the same has been buried, or from a place where the same has been deposited while awaiting burial, without authority of law, with intent to sell the same, or for the purpose of dissection, or for the purpose of procuring a reward for the return of the same, or from malice or wantonness, is punishable by imprisonment for not more than five years or by a fine not exceeding one thousand dollars, or both.*

When you cut through the verbiage, the law pretty well describes what it considers to be the only possible motives for stealing a corpse. Those are love, money, or lunacy. In fact, no matter what the criminologists will tell you, those are the only possible motives for *any* crime: love, money, or lunacy. The lunacy aspects of Section 2216 are defined in the word "wantonness" and in the phrase "for the purpose of dissection," which was probably a carry-over from the time of Dr. Frankenstein and his ilk; there were very few mad scientists running loose in the city these days. Still, there were many bedbugs in this vast metropolis for which I'd once been a public servant, and whereas

9

they didn't normally come out of the mattress in September (preferring the dog days of July and August), the possibility *did* exist that one of them had unseasonably surfaced, swiped a stiff, and then gone back to a snug hiding place in the bedsprings. If a lunatic had committed the crime, I wasn't interested. Lunatics bore me.

Love as a motive was defined in the section with the simple word "malice," which together with spite or revenge form the other side of the love coin. Perhaps this *was* simply a case of someone with a grudge against the family of the deceased, someone who'd stolen the corpse in an attempt to make tragedy even more painful than it had to be. If so, I was equally uninterested. If anything's more boring than a bedbug, it's someone with a petty grievance.

As for money, the section spelled it out with the words "with intent to sell the same," and "for the purpose of procuring a reward for the return of the same." I wasn't aware of a lively market in corpses these days, and whereas I'd handled three or four kidnappings during my years on the force, I'd never had a case in which a ransom demand had been made for a stolen body. In fact, I'd never had a case of body snatching in twenty-four years of police work, and I guess this was what caused me to tell Abner on the spot that I'd find his missing Mr. Gibson.

"But how much will you charge?" Abner asked. "For getting the body back to me by ten tomorrow morning?"

"Why ten?" I asked.

"That's when the family will be here. That's when they expect to find the body ready for viewing."

I didn't know what to tell him regarding a fee. In this city, you don't need a license to be a private detective provided you don't charge anything for your services. There is, after all, no law against being an unpaid snoop. My four previous clients had gifted me lavishly after I'd successfully concluded investigating their cases, and frankly I'd felt justified in accepting presents from them—but only because the disappointment of having solved yet another case seemed ample reason for compensation. Could I now tell Abner that *not* finding Mr. Gibson's corpse would make me a very happy man? Could I tell him that if I failed (hope springs eternal), I would not accept even a token of appreciation from him, but would instead take him to dinner in one of the city's best restaurants, where we'd drink champagne till dawn and toast the superiority of the criminal mind?

"I'm not permitted to charge a fee," I told him. "Let's simply see what happens, shall we?"

Full of perhaps childish expectations, I began.

2

A NARROW ALLEY ran between the rear of Abner's mortuary and the brick rear wall of an apartment building opposite. One end of the alley opened onto Hennessy Street, some hundred feet from the jimmied door; the other end was cut off by another brick wall at right angles to the apartment building. There was a door on this wall, as well as several lighted basement windows. I went to the door and knocked on it.

"Who is it?" a woman asked.

"Police," I said. This was a lie, but I see no harm in lying to anyone, provided it makes things easier for me. I heard a lock being turned. The door opened. The woman standing there was in her early forties, a slatternly brunette wearing a man's woolen bathrobe belted at the waist, the sleeves rolled up to accommodate the length of her own arms.

"What is it?" she said.

I showed her the gold shield, and she nodded.

"May I come in?" I asked.

She looked me over, and then stepped back from the doorway. "I was just having some breakfast," she said, and waited for me to move past her into the room, and then closed and locked the door behind me. The room was a kitchen. A table with a white enamel top was against one wall beneath two small windows opening onto the alley. A bottle of Scotch and a glass with ice cubes in it were the only things on the table; the woman apparently planned to drink her breakfast. A flowered curtain was partially drawn back over a doorway that led to a bedroom. I could see one corner of the bed. It had not been made.

"Would you like a drink?" she asked.

"Thank you, no."

"Hate to drink alone," she said, but this didn't stop her from pouring a healthy shot of Scotch over the ice cubes and downing it in a single swallow. "You sure?" she said, and poured herself another four fingers.

"Positive."

"What's the trouble?" she asked, and sat at the table, and gestured for me to take the other chair. Sipping the second drink, apparently savoring it, she watched me intently. Her eyes were green.

"I was wondering if you were here in the apartment all last night," I said.

"Why? What happened last night?" she asked.

"Routine investigation," I said. "*Were* you here?"

"Sure," she said. "Where *else* would I be? This is where I live. I'm superintendent of the building here. That's what I get paid for. To *be* here. So here's where I was."

"Did you happen to hear any traffic in the alley outside?"

"There's *always* traffic in the alley outside," she said. "Abner has dead bodies coming in every hour of the day and night."

"Did any bodies come in *last* night?"

"Who knows? I never pay attention any more. It's bad enough I *know* what's going on out there. How would you like to live next door to a funeral parlor? I see them carrying corpses in there . . ." She shivered and took another sip of Scotch. "Do you believe in ghosts?" she said.

"No."

"I do," she said. "I'm laying in bed some nights, and I think suppose one of them dead bodies takes a notion to go wandering, you know what I mean? If they're not buried yet, their spirits can go wandering. I lay there in bed, and I get the shakes. I live here all alone, you know. My husband passed on two years ago, good riddance to him. He's *one* ghost I never hope to see, I can tell you that. What's your name?"

"Benjamin Smoke."

"Mine's Connie," she said, and smiled. "Connie Brogan."

"Mrs. Brogan, can you tell me—?"

"Call me Connie," she said. "Listen, are you sure you wouldn't like just a short one? I really do hate to drink alone, Ben. Two things I hate to do are drink alone and sleep alone," she said, and smiled again. "Come on, have a quickie."

"We're not allowed to drink on duty," I said.

"Oh. Sure. Of course," she said. "Well, you won't mind if I have just another little one, will you?"

"No, no, go right ahead."

"Though, boy, I sure do hate to drink alone," she said, and poured the glass almost half full again. "Here's looking at you, Ben," she said, and drank, and then asked, "Where'd you get that scar on your cheek?"

"I got into a scrape once."

"Tough work, police work," she said. "Nobody appreciates the job cops do. You're a big fellow, though, I'll bet you can take pretty good care of yourself."

"Connie, at any time last night, did you—?"

"I like big men," she said. "The way I see it, men are supposed to be big, and women are supposed to be small. I know I don't look it in this floppy robe, but actually I'm a very dainty person. You know what my dress size is? Take a guess. Petite. I'll bet you don't believe that. That's because I'm very busty for a woman my size. But petite is what I take. Or, in some dresses, small. But never anything bigger. How old do you think I am?"

"I really couldn't say, Connie."

"Take a guess, Ben. Go on."

"Thirty-four," I said, reducing my honest estimate by a good ten years.

"*Right* on the nose!" she said. "You ought to get a job at one of them amusement parks, where they guess people's age and weight. How much do you think I weigh? Never mind looking at my bust, because that'll throw you off. I weigh one hundred and two pounds, what do you think of that? I'm five feet three inches tall and I weigh a hundred and two pounds, which is just about perfect for my size."

"What I'm interested in finding out," I said, "is whether—"

"Relax, Ben," she said. "You're a conscientious man, I admire that, but don't press so hard. What is it you want to know?"

"Did you hear any traffic outside last night?"

"Last night," she said. "Well now, let me see. I went to bed right after the eleven-o'clock news. That is, I got *ready* for bed. I take a bath every night before I go to bed. Do you take a bath before you go to bed?"

"A shower," I said. "I usually—"

"I don't like showers," she said. "I fill the tub with bubble bath, and I just lay back in it for maybe a half-hour. It's very relaxing. Anyway, I don't have a shower. All I have is a tub. It doesn't matter, 'cause I don't like showers, anyway. What do you sleep in?" she asked.

"A bed," I said.

"I mean, do you wear pajamas—or what?"

"Yes. Yes, I wear pajamas."

"I don't wear anything. I like to feel the sheets against my body. So let me see. I must've got to bed around twelve—well, maybe not *exactly* twelve, but around that time. Do you read in bed?"

"Sometimes."

"I never read in bed. I hate reading, as a matter of fact. What I do is I turn off the light, and in two or three minutes I drop off to sleep. That's *now*, of course. When my husband was alive, he used to pester me to death all night long. Anyway, I must've been sleeping like a baby by a quarter past twelve. I'm usually a very sound sleeper—that indicates a clear conscience, huh?" she said, and smiled. "But last night there was traffic outside. There's always traffic in that goddamn alley, you'd think people were dying to get in that funeral parlor." She smiled, and lifted her glass, and winked at me over it, and said, "Did you get that?"

"Yes," I said, and smiled. "Dying to get in," I said.

"You're very quick, Ben," she said. "I like bright men." She drained the glass and poured herself another drink. "So I got out of bed—*starkers*," she said, and paused for emphasis, "and took a look out the window to see what they were bringing in this time, as if I didn't know."

"What *were* they bringing in?"

"I don't know," she said. "I went right back to bed."

"Was there a car out there?"

"Yes."

"What kind of a car?"

"A Volkswagen bus."

"What year?"

"I don't know. They all look the same to me."

"What color?"

"Red-and-white. The top part was white."

"You didn't happen to notice the license plate, did you?"

"No, it was parked with the . . . you know. The *side* of it was facing the bedroom window."

"Did you notice who was driving it?"

"No, I went right back to bed."

"What time was this, would you remember?"

"Must've been three o'clock in the morning. It was still dark, I know that. Only reason I could see out there was because of the little light Abner keeps burning over his back door. Do you think he's a fag?"

"Abner?"

"Yes. I think he must be a fag. I've invited him in here for a drink on one or two occasions, and he's always said no. That indicates something to me, Ben. I'm not bragging, but most people consider me a good-looking woman. Do you think I'm a good-looking woman? You don't have to answer that," she said, and smiled. "I can tell you do."

"How long was the bus outside there?" I asked.

"I couldn't say. I went right back to bed again. I have to get up early in the morning, you know. We've got a porter working here in the building, and he's supposed to put out the garbage cans for pickup in the morning, but if I'm not there to supervise him, it never gets done. Nobody takes pride in his work any more, Ben. That's why I admire you so much. The job you're doing."

"What time did you get up this morning?" I asked.

"Usual time. Six A.M., rain or shine. The porter gets here at six-thirty, and by then I've usually thrown on a pair of dungarees and a sweatshirt, and I'm out there to supervise him putting out the cans. Takes him a half-hour or so, and then I usually have a glass of orange juice and go back to bed."

"Is that what you did this morning?"

"That's what I do every morning except Sunday, when there's no garbage collection."

"Was the bus gone when you woke up at six?"

"Yep. Gone with the wind. What time is it now, anyway?"

I looked at my watch. "It's almost ten," I said.

"Where *does* the day go?" she said, and smiled. "I'd better put some clothes on," she said. "Before you start getting ideas. Me sitting around in just a robe."

I stood up, put the chair back in place under the table, and said, "You've been very helpful, Connie. Thank you."

"What is it you're investigating, anyway?" she asked. "Sit down, Ben, don't be in such a hurry. I can tell you're a very active man, but that's no reason to go running off."

"I've got some other stops," I said.

"What time do you think you'll be through?" she asked.

"I have no idea."

"Give me a call," she said, "huh? Maybe we can have a drink together. When you're off duty, I mean. It's 555-2368. Very easy to remember. Do you think you can remember it?"

"I'll remember it," I said.

"I'll bet you have a very retentive memory," she said. "Don't forget, okay? 555-2368. Even if you're through late tonight, that'll be okay, you can call whenever you're through, okay? You might feel like having a drink after a hard day's work, who knows? I'll be here."

"Thanks again," I said, and left.

3

THE ADDRESS Abner had given me for Rhoda Gibson, widow of the departed corpse, was in a row of brownstones close to one of the city's five universities, and about ten blocks from his funeral home. I located the building, and then drove around the block twice before I found a parking space. The car I drive is a 1973 450SL Mercedes-Benz, a gift from a grateful German countess for whom I'd recovered $700,000 worth of jewels stolen from her hotel room. I always leave it unlocked when I park it on any city street. The steering wheel locks when the ignition key is removed, and so I'm never worried that someone's going to drive off with the car. But if a booster wants to steal my radio, I'd rather he simply opened an unlocked door, instead of slashing my convertible top to steal the radio, anyway.

1214 Matthews was the third brownstone in from Cooper Street, a stately three-story building with wide white steps leading up to the entrance door. As I approached the building, I saw a bearded young giant of a man inserting a key into the outer vestibule door at the top of the steps. He was wearing dungaree trousers, a pullover sweater, and track shoes. His hair and his beard were red. Since he seemed to fit the description Abner had given me of Jeffrey Gibson, the dead man's son, and since he was inserting a key into the door of Rhoda Gibson's residence, I came to a not spectacularly brilliant conclusion, started up the steps, and said, "Mr. Gibson?"

Mr. Gibson (or whoever he was) turned from the door. I

recognized the look in his eyes an instant before it was too late. The look was one of total panic. His right hand yanked up the ribbed bottom of his sweater, I saw the butt of a revolver sticking up out of the waistband of his dungarees, and then the revolver was in his hand. I was at a decided disadvantage, being two steps lower than the gun and the man. I hurled myself up and forward, grabbing him around the knees and knocking him off balance, and together we came rolling down the steps and onto the sidewalk.

If there's one thing I detest, it's any kind of sweaty combat. The day I'd had my cheek permanently adorned, I'd struggled for a good ten minutes in embrace with a man holding a six-inch-long switchblade knife and intent on taking out my liver and intestines, though he wasn't licensed to practice medicine in this city. I'd clung to his wrist for what seemed an eternity, and had managed—but only *after* he'd slashed open my cheek—to bring a knee up into his groin, and finally to take the knife away from him. I had learned elementary judo at the police academy, but as soon as the cheek healed, I began studying the art in earnest. I still don't consider myself an expert, but I know how to kill a man with a swift, hard, edge-of-the-hand blow across the bridge of his nose, or a sharp, two-fingered jab at his Adam's apple. I also know how to break a man's arm or leg with a minimum of effort, an economy of motion, and a power usually generated by his own physical thrust. I prefer my fights short and sweet, and preferably not at all. Real-life fights are not like those you see in the movies. Two stalwarts do not stand there punching at each other until one or the other falls senseless and bleeding to the ground. Instead, there's usually utter confusion, a tangle of arms and legs, broken knuckles when bare fists collide with unyielding skulls, kicks, grunts, fingers clawing at eyes and hair, attempts to strangle, headlocks, biting—a totally animalistic display better suited to a pair of moose locking horns in the north woods. I've learned three things about street fights. (1) Unless it's absolutely necessary, never start up with a man who has nothing to lose. He'll kill you. (2) Get it over with fast, the quicker the better. (3) Never expect help from a passing stranger; this is the city.

As Jeffrey Gibson (or whoever he was) struggled to get the pistol in firing position while I kept a tight grip on his wrist, and as *I* struggled to get my free hand where I could hurt him, perhaps two dozen pedestrians walked past us on the sidewalk, intent on getting to wherever they were going. The pistol was a .32-caliber Smith & Wesson, meaning he had six chances to do me in. I didn't know why he was so intent on having me dead, but panic is a good enough reason for murdering someone, and panic was stampeding his eyes like a herd of wild buffalo. My right hand still clenched around his wrist, and holding his flailing arm out and away from me, I managed to clutch a handful of groin, and I squeezed hard, and he let out a wounded shriek and fell back on the pavement. I grabbed his wrist in both hands now, and battered his gun hand repeatedly against the sidewalk until he released his grip on the weapon. Straddling him, I slapped him across the face, and then slapped him again and again, humiliating him, breaking his will to continue the fight. I was sweating, and breathing very hard.

"All right?" I said.

He didn't answer. I brought back my hand to slap him again, and he twisted his head away, and closed his eyes like a child expecting punishment from a wrathful father, and then he nodded and said, "Please . . . no more."

I got to my feet. He was writhing on the pavement, his hands clutching his abused genitals. I picked up the .32, tucked it into my belt, helped him to his feet, and sat him down on the bottom step of the stoop. "Are you Jeffrey Gibson?" I said.

"Yes," he answered.

"What the hell's the matter with you, Gibson? Why'd you pull a gun on me?"

"You *know* why," he said.

"No, I don't."

"Who are you?" he said.

"Who'd you *think* I was?" I said.

"One of them."

"One of *who*?"

"The men who killed my father."

"What men?"

"I don't know who they are."

"What makes you think someone killed him?"

"I know."

"*How* do you know?"

"They threatened to do it, and now they've done it."

"Why'd they threaten to kill him?"

"Because he owed them money."

"How much money?"

"Twelve thousand dollars. My father was a gambler," Jeffrey said, and then raised his head and grimaced, and said, "A very *bad* gambler."

"Tell me," I said.

Anthony Gibson had been not only a bad gambler, according to his son, but actually the worst kind of gambler. I have very little respect for people who *play* for a living. In my book, the world is divided between the Players and the Workers. Thieves and gamblers are Players. So are prize fighters, entire football teams, tennis champions, golf pros, and men gifted with the talent of tossing a dart a hundred yards across a pub to hit the bull's-eye in the center of a board. Even *expert* gamblers, those who've made a science of figuring the odds, are still only Players. But the worst sort of gambler is the man who'll bet on *anything*, the man who actually believes Lady Luck is controlling the outcome of any given event.

Anthony Gibson had been such a man. He would bet on a cockroach race or the eventuality of a snowstorm in July. He would bet that Jack Benny's real name had been Myron Fenster-

macher; he would bet that any given blonde walking down the
street was in reality a brunette; he would bet that on the twelfth
of October, in the city of Rangoon, a rat would bite a Buddhist
monk on the backside. Such a man is a fool. He's a bigger fool if
his income can't keep up with his wild wagers. Anthony Gibson
had worked as an advertising copywriter for the firm of Haley,
Blake & Bonatti, and had earned a yearly salary of $47,500,
which he'd squandered on ponies, crap games, card games, lot-
tery tickets, and bets as to whether or not the moon would rise
over Seattle at 7:10 P.M. on Monday night. His wife and recent
widow, Rhoda, ran an interior-decorating business that brought
in another thirty thousand a year—much of which Gibson begged
or badgered from her to get him out of one gambling debt or
another.

A month back, the phone at the Gibson residence had begun
ringing with calls for Gibson *père*. The calls sometimes came in
the middle of the night. Gibson would hold a brief conversation
with whoever was on the other end of the line, and then instantly
get out of bed and go down to the living room, where he sometimes sat drinking till dawn. During one of those early-hour calls,
Jeffrey had picked up the extension and eavesdropped on the
conversation. He learned that his father owed twelve thousand
dollars for an I.O.U. he'd signed during a poker game in July.
His father promised the caller he was working on raising the
money, and that all he needed was a little more time, and would
they please stop phoning in the middle of the night, as they were
beginning to alarm his family. The man on the other end said the
family would be even *more* alarmed in the future if Gibson
didn't come up with the cash damn soon. Toward the end of
August, two men arrived at the house shortly after dinner. One
of them was about my size, with a scar on his face, which was
why Jeffrey had mistaken me for him not five minutes ago, and
drawn the revolver—in self-defense, of course. Jeffrey overheard
the terse discussion they had with his father. The men told Gib-

son that if he didn't pay the twelve thousand dollars before September 8, they would kill him. As best as he could recall, the visit had been sometime during the weekend of August 24. Today was Monday, September 9, and his father had met with a fatal automobile accident last night on his way home. Jeffrey *had* to assume the "accident" had been arranged by the men who'd been dunning his father. Nor did he believe they were finished yet. On their warning visit, *he* had been the one who'd opened the door to let them into the house; he had seen them, he knew what they looked like. He was certain they would come after him next.

I listened to Jeffrey's theory with only polite interest. In the code of men who accept markers from losing gamblers, the debt *must* be paid in one way or another. But these men are in business, and they realize just as certainly as any other businessmen that if they kill the person who owes them money, the money will never be collected. Better to break his arm a little, or rearrange his nose. Homicide is the last resort of creditors; the money owed will never be retrieved. At the same time, it is an extremely convincing reminder to *future* I.O.U. writers. When murder *does* become necessary, however, it's usually done more dramatically, so that there'll be no mistake about who ordered the execution or why. An automobile accident? This hardly seemed the style of men trying to teach an object lesson. If you want to warn other gamblers that they can't welsh with impunity, you don't commit a murder that might be misconstrued as an accident. And even if someone *had* tampered with Gibson's automobile, or forced him off the road, or otherwise arranged for his collision, his son's fears seemed unreasonable. Rarely will underworld creditors knock off a debtor and then go after his family as well. That's merely waste motion, and Players like to conserve their energy.

I asked Jeffrey where I might find his mother, and he gave me the address of her place of business uptown. This bothered me immediately. Granted Mrs. Gibson owned a business, granted she needed to put all her time and energy into running it, especially since her late spouse had done his utmost to squander her earnings as well as his own, it nonetheless seemed passing strange that she would go to work on the day after her husband had been killed in an automobile accident. In my years as a cop, I'd run across a great many self-possessed women, but never had I met a grieving widow who'd carted her dead husband's body to a funeral home, left instructions on how to dress and package it, and then gone off to business as usual. Rhoda Gibson's sang-froid seemed a bit unusual, to say the least.

I had no wish to carry around with me a pistol that might have been a stolen one, so I returned the Smith & Wesson to Jeffrey, with the suggestion that he try not to shoot himself in the foot with it. It was twenty-five minutes to eleven. I went back to where I'd parked the Mercedes, and drove east toward the television-repair shop of Henry Garavelli.

4

HENRY WAS WEARING blue coveralls with yellow stitching over the right-hand flap pocket, GTV for Garavelli Television. I shook his hand with a curious feeling of paternal pride. I'd known him for more than five years now, having first made his acquaintance when he was eighteen and a member of a street gang euphemistically named The Cardinals, S.A.C., the "S.A.C." standing for "Social and Athletic Club." Most of the gang's socializing had been done on tenement rooftops with willing teenage "debs," and most of the athletics required breaking heads with tire chains, slashing faces with ripped-off car aerials, and stabbing with switchblades or shooting with Saturday-night specials the members of "spic clubs," this being a time when the emergence of Puerto Ricans as something more than second-class citizens was causing all sorts of nationalistic fervor to rise in the breasts of fourth-generation Italians eager to protect their turf. I thought I'd seen the last of the street gangs in the late forties and early fifties, but in 1969, when I met Henry for the first time, the resurgence was beginning. By the time I quit the force, it had again become a full-blown plague upon the city.

Henry was now twenty-three years old, and he had served three and a half years in prison because I sent him there after I caught him holding up a grocery store. Henry was nineteen at the time, having graduated from his bopping street gang to shooting heroin into his arms, thirty dollars' worth a day, which came to two hundred and ten dollars a week—a long habit to support unless you are burglarizing, mugging, and otherwise supplementing your nonexistent income by holding up markets, tailor shops, liquor stores, and the like. Henry never admitted to anything but the grocery-store stickup, but that was enough to gross him a ten-year sentence for a first offense, reduced to three and a half by the Parole Board after he proved to be an ideal prisoner.

As an ex-cop, I know that most prisons are medieval ratholes, criminal and homosexual training grounds, and dehumanizing, brutalizing conclaves in the midst of a society that claims to be humane, idealistic, and aspiring to greatness. The miracle of Henry Garavelli was that he'd not only survived the prison system, he had benefited from it as well. To begin with, he'd kicked the habit, no small feat in a correctional institution where drugs were as easily, if not more readily, available than they were on the street. He had *not* learned a trade (unless you want to believe that working in the prison laundry prepared him for gainful occupation in the world outside), but he *had* completed his high school education through a correspondence course, and upon his release in the early part of 1973, had immediately enrolled in a television-repair school.

There are skeptics who believe that television repairmen are even bigger thieves than armed robbers, but the fact remains that Henry Garavelli started his own business after he got out of school, and had been earning a good and honest living for the past sixteen months. The peculiar thing about it all was that he was grateful to me for having busted him. He considered the bust fortuitous, perhaps because too many of his "luckier" friends, those who'd never been arrested, were still at the same old stand—mugging, stealing, and begging to support habits as long as the subway system. I'd busted him only because he'd held up a grocery store; I was a cop doing my job. On the other hand, Henry considered himself in my debt, and would go miles out of his way—as he'd done only last year, when I was searching for a lead to the countess's missing baubles—to bring me information or to perform legwork that would help in an investigation. He'd enjoyed himself enormously on that single case he'd worked with me, had felt, in fact, somewhat like a free-lance, super-secret agent without whose assistance the countess would have gone back to Munich minus her treasures.

The age difference between us was twenty years and more, but I doubt if it contributed anything toward understanding the father-son nature of our relationship. I'm a bachelor, of course, without children of my own, so perhaps that explains part of it. Henry's own father was killed in a bar fight when Henry was eight, and perhaps that explains yet another part of it. Maybe Henry, grateful to me, was only emulating me when he helped me recover those jewels, and maybe I was only teaching Henry the tricks of the trade—passing on the tradition, so to speak. A Freudian might also discover significance in the fact that Henry had helped a former cop, even though cops in general had made his life miserable when he was a kid, even though a cop had finally sent him to prison, where cops disguised as screws had made his life even more miserable. Who knows? We liked each other. We trusted each other. That was enough.

Blue-eyed like a Milanese, short and dark, with the curly black hair of a Neapolitan, and a nose any Roman would have been proud to call his own, Henry got to the point as directly as a Sicilian.

"How come you ain't been around?" he said.

"I've been away," I said. "Vacation."

"So you're back, ain't you? So whyn't you give me a ring, I'll lend you my assistance on a case or two."

"What's the matter? Business slow?"

"Terrible. Money's tight. Used to be a guy had a little something wrong with the set, he'd rush to have it fixed. Nowadays, thanks to that jerk in the White House, nobody gets his television fixed unless there's no picture at *all* on the tube. I'm thinking of going back to sticking up grocery stores," he said, and grinned.

"Good idea," I said. "Unless you'd prefer going on the earie for me again."

"Ah?" he said, and raised his eyebrows expectantly.

"A body was stolen from Abner Boone's mortuary on Hennessy Street at around three A.M. I don't know who ripped it off or why. Can you listen around? Maybe it's unusual enough to have caused a rumble."

"A *dead* body, you mean?" Henry said.

"Mm. Man named Anthony Gibson, died in an automobile accident last night. His son thinks he was murdered, but I'm not sure about that yet—even though he owed twelve thousand bucks to some hoods who were putting the arm on him."

"Anybody I know?"

"All I've got is a loose description, Henry. One of them is supposed to look something like me, about my height and weight, scar on his face. The other one is short and dark."

"You think they might be the ones who snatched the body?"

"It's a possibility. Gibson owed them twelve thousand dollars. They couldn't get it from *him* when he was alive, so maybe they plan on getting it from the *family* now that he's dead."

"Like a kidnapping, huh? Only the victim is a stiff."

"Exactly."

"In which case, they'll pretty soon be asking for twelve grand in ransom."

"*If* they're the ones who did the job."

"I like it," Henry said. "When did Gibson write that marker?"

"Sometime in July. At a poker game."

"Where?"

"I don't know."

"How soon you need this?"

"Right away."

Henry looked at his watch. "It's only a quarter past eleven," he said. "Half the hoods I know are still asleep. Where can I reach you later?"

"You can leave a message at my apartment. Have you still got the number?"

"Tattooed on my brain," Henry said, and grinned again.

5

THE PRECINCT commanded by Captain Ferdinand Cupera was one the city had overlooked in its recent, frantic rebuilding and/or renovation program. This meant that it had been on the same spot since 1927, the year in which it was built. And despite an annual interior coat of apple-green paint, there was no hiding the building's decrepitude. The thing to remember about any police station is that it's used twenty-four hours a day by rotating teams of detectives, uniformed policemen, clerks, criminals, and victims. The furniture, the water coolers, the typewriters, the telephones, the holding cells, the lockers, the Coca-Cola machine, and the toilets never get a rest. Given this constant use (and abuse), it's a wonder *any* of them—including the new sleekly modern yellow-brick precincts the city had spent a fortune to construct—managed to survive at all.

I climbed the broad flat steps leading to the double wooden entrance doors, green globes flanking the steps, the numeral "12" lettered on each in white. A patrolman stopped me just outside the muster room, and I flashed the gold, and he said, "Anyone special you want to see, Loot?" I told him I was there to see Captain Cupera, and then I walked in toward the familiar muster desk, identical to the one in the precinct uptown, where I'd spent twenty-four years of my professional life. A sergeant sat behind the high wooden desk, reading a magazine. I stopped at the brass railing in front of the desk, saw the sign advising all visitors that they must state their business to the sergeant, saw the Miranda-Escobedo rights poster printed in English and Spanish and tacked to the wall behind the desk, saw the electrical board with warning lights that would flash red if any of the holding-cell doors were open, saw the board with keys on it, saw the sergeant's battery of telephones, and the duty chart, and the calendar and the muster book open on the worn, smooth top of the desk, saw all of these things and felt not the faintest trace of nostalgia.

The sergeant looked up. "Help you?" he said.

I showed him my shield, told him who I was, and said I would like to see the captain. He lifted a telephone, held a brief conversation with Coop, and then asked me if I knew the way. I told him I did, and went across the muster room, past the Dispatcher's Office and the Clerical Office and the swing room, where a patrolman was sitting in his undershirt sipping hot coffee from a mug, his uniform jacket draped over the back of a wooden chair. I knocked on the frosted-glass door marked COMMANDING OFFICER.

"Come in," Coop called, and I opened the door and went into his office. It was larger than the one I'd occupied on the second floor of the building uptown. This was proper and fitting, since I'd commanded only eighteen detectives, whereas Coop was in charge of an entire precinct—two hundred cops in all, including the plainclothesmen, over whom he had authority superseding the detective-lieutenant's. He was sitting behind a desk piled high with paperwork. There were four barred windows in the room. Two of them were open to the mild September breeze. A shaft of sunlight speared the armchair in front of his desk. He rose the moment I entered, extended his hand, and said, "Long time no see." His voice still carried the faintest trace of a Spanish accent, though he had come from Puerto Rico nearly forty years before. "Sit down," he said. "You want some coffee?"

"Thanks," I said, "I'm in a hurry."

"You just *got* here," he said, looking mildly offended.

"Coop," I said, "I want to report a missing corpse."

"A missing *what*?"

"Corpse."

"Ha ha," he said mirthlessly.

"Illegally removed from the premises of one Abner Boone, 3418 Hennessy Street at or about three A.M. Mr. Boone is an undertaker."

"You're serious?" Coop said.

"I'm serious. The deceased answers to the name of Anthony Gibson, forty-two years old—"

"Just a second," Coop said, and began writing.

"Five-eleven, a hundred and eighty-five pounds, dark hair, brown eyes."

"What's your interest in this stiff?"

"I promised to get it back before ten tomorrow morning."

"Benny, if you want to keep playing cops and robbers, why don't you come back on the force?" Coop said. He was the only man in the world who called me Benny. A lot of women called me Benny, but that was forgivable. I tolerated the diminutive when Coop used it only because he gave it such a distinctive Old World twist, making it sound more like "Baynee."

"Well, this looks like an interesting case," I said.

"They *all* look interesting," Coop said.

"There've only been four so far. That's not a lot."

"That's enough. Anyway, is what you're doing legal? Don't you need a license to do what you're doing?"

"I'm merely helping people with seemingly difficult problems, Coop."

"I'm sure you need a license for that," Coop said. "I could probably lock you up, you know that?"

"Don't lock me up, okay? Just do a favor for me."

"What favor?"

"So far, I've got only one thing to go on. The body was carried off in a red-and-white Volkswagen bus."

"What year?" Coop said. He was writing again.

"The lady didn't know."

"What lady?"

"The lady who saw it."

"So what do you want?"

"First, I'd like a look at your hot-car sheet . . ."

"There's one in the squadroom upstairs, and another one outside in the muster room."

"And then I'd appreciate it if you called Auto and asked them for an up-to-date."

"Okay."

In this city, the Automobile Squad puts out a daily mimeographed bulletin listing all the cars stolen the day before. Two copies of it are supposed to be delivered to all the precincts in the city at seven-thirty each morning—one going to the Detective Division, and the other posted in the muster room so that the uniformed men can take a look at it before going out to relieve on post. The sheet rarely arrives before noon, though, making it relatively stale by the time the next shift goes out at three forty-five. Coop had just agreed to call Auto for their most recent reports on stolen vehicles.

"What else?" he said.

"That's it."

"Okay. If you want to check the sheet, I'll get on the phone to Auto."

"Thank you, Coop."

In the muster room outside, I looked over the mimeographed hot-car sheet. Six Beetles had been stolen the day before, but only one VW bus—and it was blue. I went back to Coop's office. He was shaking his head as I came in.

"Nothing," he said. "You're out of luck."

"Will you keep me posted if it shows later?"

"I can't call Auto every ten minutes," Coop said.

"Just give them another ring before you go home."

"Benny," he said, "the Police Department is not being run for the benefit of a retired lieutenant."

"How's Consuela?" I said.

"Consuela's fine, don't change the subject."

"And the kids?"

"The kids are fine, too."

"Will you call Auto later?"

"I'll call them."

"Thank you, Coop," I said.

"Yeah, yeah," he answered, and waved me out.

I asked the desk sergeant for change of a quarter, and then went to the pay phone in the swing room. Two patrolmen were drinking coffee and exchanging atrocity stories about their respective beats. I closed the door to the booth and dialed my home number. The phone rang twice before it was picked up.

"'Allo," Lisette said.

"It's me," I said. "Were there any calls?"

"Maria calls," Lisette said. "You are to call her back."

"Anyone else?"

"No one. Will you be home for dinner?"

"I don't think so," I said.

"Then I will leave at five," she said.

"Lisette, I'd like you to stay tonight, if that's all right with you. I may be getting some calls."

She was silent for a moment. Then she said, "Are you doing it again?"

"Yes," I said, "I'm doing it again."

We were both referring to the fact that I'd taken on another case. Lisette sighed.

"Will you stay?" I asked.

"*Pour sûr*, I will stay," she said, and hung up.

I tried Maria's number, and got her answering service, which I always consider a waste of ten cents. I told the nasal-voiced girl on the other end that Benjamin Smoke had called and that I would try to get back to Miss Hochs later, but she was not to count on it. When I came out of the booth, one of the patrolmen was telling a story about a black numbers runner. I went through the muster room and down the precinct steps. There was a parking summons on my windshield. I put it in the glove compartment alongside a dozen similar summonses. Then I inserted the key into the ignition, but I didn't start the car. With my hands on the wheel, I stared straight ahead through the windshield and felt the first vague stirrings of hope. I'd touched all bases, but until I heard something further from either Henry or Coop, I had nothing concrete to go on. I intended to talk to Rhoda Gibson, of course, in an attempt to find out whether or not she'd been contacted by anyone demanding ransom for the return of her husband's corpse. The body had been swiped at three A.M., and it was now close to twelve noon, and nine hours was a long enough time for the kidnapper (if such he was) to get busy on the telephone. But if there'd been no demand . . .

My hand was shaking as I twisted the ignition key. I tried to tell myself the excitement was premature. Coop or Henry would most surely come up with a lead, and *this* case would end as all the others had. But I was smiling as I drove uptown to talk to Rhoda Gibson.

6

I REACHED her office at twelve-thirty, just as she was preparing to leave. I told her my name and identified myself as a working policeman investigating the possibility that her husband's death had been something more than accidental. I was there to ask if anyone had made a ransom demand, but at the same time I couldn't reveal that her husband's corpse had been spirited away, so to speak. Abner Boone was, after all, my client. Inherent in our verbal agreement was the understanding that the Gibson family would never learn of the theft; if all went well (or badly, depending on how you looked at it), they'd simply arrive at the mortuary tomorrow morning and find a neatly dressed body waiting to be eulogized and buried.

"I can't talk to you right now," Rhoda said. "I'm in a dreadful hurry, Lieutenant, I hope you'll excuse me."

"Mrs. Gibson," I said, "your husband—"

"I'm sorry," she said, "but an antiques dealer called me not five minutes ago, and I've *got* to get there right away."

"Where's that?"

"Wilson Street," she said.

"I'll drive you over. We can talk on the way."

"Well . . . all right," she said. "But please let's hurry."

Rhoda Gibson was an attractive woman just this side of forty, her black hair cut in a shingle bob. Her eyes were brown, she wore no make-up. She was dressed in what I assumed to be her usual working garb—a pale-blue pants suit, a flowered-silk blouse under it, stock tie knotted into a bow at the throat, low-heeled blue patent shoes. She put on a light topcoat before we left the office, and we went downstairs and walked toward where I'd parked the Mercedes. As we drove crosstown, I asked her if she thought there might have been anything suspicious about her husband's accident.

"Why would I think that?" she said.

"Your son seems to think so. He told me—"

"When did you talk to my son?"

"Earlier today."

"Where?"

"Outside your house on Matthews Street. He was carrying a pistol."

"A pistol? Where on earth did he get a pistol?"

"They're very easy to come by in this city. Or *any* city, for that matter. He's very frightened, Mrs. Gibson. He thinks your husband was killed. And he thinks whoever did it isn't quite finished yet. Are *you* frightened?"

"No. Why should I be?"

"Your son said—"

"I wouldn't take anything he told you seriously."

"*Did* some men come to your house and threaten your husband?"

"Yes, but that was par for the course. A week didn't go by without someone demanding money from Tony."

"Then you don't believe those men had anything to do with his accident?"

"I don't know," Rhoda said. "And I don't care. Would you like to know something? I'm glad he's dead."

She said this just as I parked in front of the antique shop. I pulled up the handbrake and turned on the seat to look at her. Her face was expressionless.

"Why are you glad?" I asked.

"I just am."

"No reason?"

"Two *hundred* of them," she said, and opened the door on the curb side and got out of the car.

I looked at my watch. It was twenty minutes to one, and there was in the streets that sort of calm that can settle unexpectedly on the city at any hour of the day, exaggerated by an afternoon clarity of light that gave a sharp-edged luminosity to people and things, as though they'd been frozen in still photographs taken by an expert photographer. We walked to the shop in silence. Rhoda pushed open the door, and a bell tinkled, and a tall, long-faced, lavender-haired woman came from the back of the shop and greeted her with an exuberant "Rhoda! You sure got here fast!"

"Have you still got the lamps?" Rhoda said.

She didn't bother to introduce me, even though the woman with the tinted hair was studying me speculatively. We were surrounded by expensive antiques—a Welsh dresser circa 1800, an Early American gate-leg table, an English carved-oak china cabinet, a set of early-nineteenth-century ladder-back chairs, a hand-pegged trestle table, a solid-cherry William and Mary highboy. In the midst of this musty clutter, Rhoda suddenly looked cool and sleek—and deadly. My heart lurched just a trifle in disappointment. I don't ordinarily believe in hunches. Hunches are for television cops. But then again, neither am I normally presented with a lady who tells me she has two hundred reasons for rejoicing over her husband's death, a lady who doesn't bother to mention to someone who greets her on a first-name basis that dear old Tony died in a car crash last night, a lady who inquires instead, "Have you still got the lamps?"

The lamps in question were a pair of magnificent Dresden Rose lamps of the Victorian period, the shades and fonts of hand-blown opalescent glass, and the trimmings and pedestals of antique brass. While Rhoda and the lady with the lavender hair discussed the suitability of the lamps for the room Rhoda was decorating, and then haggled over the price, and then agreed upon a compromise price, I thought about my further approach to the widow of Anthony Gibson. I'd discovered over the years that if I wanted to know something, all I had to do was say "Tell me" in a sympathetic, undemanding way. The Tell Me Ploy didn't always work with guilty parties (perpetrators, as they're known in the trade), in that anything an ax murderer said was generally a lie. But I decided I'd risk it on Rhoda, even though I'd *already* asked her why she was glad her husband was dead, and had only been told there were two hundred reasons. So I waited while the lavender-haired woman with the tall body and the long face affixed a pair of red SOLD tags to the lamps, and then I politely bid her good day while she again looked at me speculatively, perhaps wondering what the married Mrs. Gibson was doing on a Monday afternoon with a modest, good-looking devil of a man who was not her husband.

Rhoda opened the door of the shop, and the bell tinkled, and we stepped out onto the sidewalk and walked to the car. On the way crosstown again, I said, "A little while ago you mentioned you were glad your husband's dead."

"That's right," she said.

"But you didn't tell me why."

"That's right, I didn't."

"Tell me," I said.

As I'd surmised, there were not two hundred reasons. There were only two:

(1) Rhoda Gibson was sick to death of her husband's gambling, drinking, and whoring. Yes, the now-deceased Mr. Gibson had fancied himself quite a swordsman, and among other payoffs Rhoda had been required to make in the past was one demanded by an enterprising photographer who'd taken pictures of Tony and a black prostitute in a series of somewhat compromising positions.

(2) Tony had left behind a sizable insurance policy, the premiums on which the redoubtable Rhoda had maintained during the twenty-odd years of their stormy marriage. Had Anthony Gibson died a natural death, Rhoda would have collected a hundred thousand bucks in cool American currency. But the policy carried a double-indemnity rider, and since Tony had been foresighted enough to die in an automobile accident, Rhoda could now look forward to *two* hundred thousand as balm for her all-consuming grief. Once she collected, she planned to move back to her native state, California, where she would open a new business, spend part of the day decorating the homes of *nouveaux riches* actors, and the rest of the day swimming and playing tennis.

"Tony *hated* playing tennis," she said.

"Mm," I said.

"So now I've told you," she said. "And now, naturally, you're going to start thinking *I* arranged for someone to saw his axle almost in half, or force him off the road, or lock his steering wheel, or whatever the hell."

"That sounds a bit too obvious, doesn't it?"

"Policemen always look for the obvious," she said.

"*Was* his axle almost sawed in half?"

"I have no idea. The car is at a place called Geraldi Body and Fender on Lowell Place. You can check it there, if you like."

"About someone forcing him off the road . . ."

"I don't know how he happened to hit that pillar," Rhoda said. "For all I know, he was drunk. As usual."

"Mrs. Gibson," I said, "on the off chance that your husband's death *was* something more than accidental . . ." (and this is where I began to lie again) "people who commit crimes of violence will often call the family of the deceased to gloat or to taunt or to—"

"No," she said. "No one's called me."

"Not since the time of the accident last night?"

"That's right. No one. No one's even called to offer condolences. Would you like to know why? Because Anthony Gibson was a *bum*. Period."

7

HE DIDN'T LOOK like a bum in the color photograph she gave me. The picture had been taken outside the Matthews Street brownstone. Gibson was standing beside a sidewalk tree in new leaf. He was wearing a pale-blue turtleneck, a blue blazer, gray slacks, and black loafers. His dark hair was windblown, his eyes were crinkled in a smile, his teeth were very white. He looked handsome and self-assured, a man without a trouble in the universe. I put the photograph in my notebook, and then, hoping Coop was not out to lunch, found a stationery store and called him from a booth near the cigar counter. The desk sergeant told me his phone was busy and asked me to wait. I waited.

When he came on the line, he sounded harried and a trifle breathless. "All hell's breaking loose around here," he said. "We have a guy upstairs who blew off his wife's face with a shotgun."

"Then I don't suppose you got a chance to call Auto."

"I called them, Benny. No red-and-white VW buses. Anyway, your case is already closed."

"What do you mean?" I said.

"We found the body."

"What?"

"We found a corpse that fits the description you gave me."

"Where'd you find it?"

"In an empty lot on Tyrone and Seventh."

"Forty-two years old, five-eleven—?"

"Yeah, yeah, about a hundred eighty-five pounds, dark hair."

"Clothed or naked?"

"Clothed. A blue pin-striped suit."

"Where's the corpse now?"

"It *was* at the morgue."

"Saint Augustine's?"

"Yes, but your friend probably picked it up already."

"What friend?"

"The undertaker. I called him the minute we found the stiff."
Coop hesitated. "Did I do something wrong, Benny?" he asked.
"I didn't cut you out of a fee or anything, did I?"

"No, no," I said. "Actually, you did a very good job."

"Okay," he said, "I got to run. Take care, huh?"

As soon as he hung up, I called Abner's funeral home. He answered the phone on the third ring.

"Hello?" he said.

"Abner, it's Benjamin Smoke."

"Ah," he said, "good. I've been trying to reach you. Your
housekeeper—"

"I understand Mr. Gibson has been located."

"He has indeed," Abner said. "I've just returned from the hospital mortuary, in fact."

"It *was* Mr. Gibson then?"

"No question. I've already sent one of my drivers to pick up
the body."

"Well then, everything seems to have worked out well," I said.

"Yes. I can't thank you enough, Lieutenant."

"Don't thank me," I said. "Thank the Police Department."

"Well, you were the one who alerted them. I must confess I
was a bit irritated when Captain Cupera called. I hadn't gone to
the police in the first place because I was—"

"I'm sure he handled it discreetly, Abner."

"Oh yes, most discreetly. I have no complaints, Lieutenant,
none at all. In fact, I'd appreciate it if you sent me your bill immediately so that—"

ED McBAIN

"No need for that, Abner. I hardly did anything at all."

"Well . . . thank you again, Lieutenant."

"Goodbye, Abner," I said, and hung up.

I deposited another dime, called Henry Garavelli's shop, and got no answer there. I then called Maria, got *her* instead of her service this time, and asked if she would care to join me for a late lunch. Maria said she'd be delighted. I made more change at the cigar counter, went back to wait outside the booth—which a fat lady in a flowered bonnet had usurped during my brief absence—and then called my apartment and told Lisette where I'd be if Henry tried to reach me. I didn't want him to continue flogging a dead horse, so to speak.

I felt rather odd as I walked back to the car.

There was neither the disappointment of having cracked a case, nor the joy I'd hoped for in failure. There was, in fact, nothing at all.

8

MARIA HOCHS had inherited blond hair and blue eyes from her father, an exquisite profile from her mother, and hips and breasts that could claim ancestral influence both Latin and Teutonic. Her long legs were strictly American. She was a beauty, and bright besides, with an infectious sense of humor and a self-confident ease about herself as a woman. She was thirty-four years old, still taking acting lessons, still making the rounds daily, still working showcases in little theaters scattered throughout the city, still hoping to become an internationally famous star. One of the things I had to overlook about Maria was her interminable chatter about acting. Maria was always "up for a part." Maria had always been "called back" to read again, Maria was always certain she'd have won the coveted role if only they hadn't "really been looking for" a redhead. Or a brunette. Or someone shorter. Or someone taller. Or someone older. Or younger. Or black. Or Chinese. I suffered through her eternal optimism only because she was more mature and realistic concerning other aspects of her life.

She was now telling me about an audition she'd had that morning for a role in a television soap, while simultaneously demolishing a large order of *osso bucco*, a side order of *spaghetti all'aglio*, and a plate of *rugula* salad. I'd chosen this particular restaurant for our lunch date because I knew it wasn't frequented by Mafia hoods. In my estimation, southern Italians know nothing at all about good food, and the *worst* cuisine in the world is Sicilian. If I know the Mafia eats someplace, I stay away from it because (a) I might get ptomaine poisoning, and (b) I might get shot. One never knows when the Family goons will decide to uphold their ridiculous code of honor by opening fire on two cheap thieves at a nearby table. Since I trust no one's aim but my own, I normally try to avoid a rain of bullets fired by a cockeyed button man.

"I worked with the director in Ogunquit two summers ago," Maria was saying, "so I think I've got a really good shot at the part." She rolled her lovely blue eyes, stuffed some dangling spaghetti into her mouth and said, "I've got my fingers crossed." She was wearing a low-cut print better suited to the Costa Smeralda than Little Italy, emerald earrings dangling from her ear lobes—not for nothing had Maria Hochs lived for two years with a stockbroker later indicted for fraud. "The part is a nurse," she said. "Do you think I'd make a good nurse?"

"I think you'd make a fantastic nurse," I said.

"I'm serious, Ben."

"So am I. You've got all the qualifications. Sympathy, compassion, tenderness, an air of efficiency, and a beautiful behind."

Henry Garavelli came into the restaurant just then, immediately located our table, and walked over to it.

"Excuse me for interrupting your meal," he said.

"Sit down, Henry," I said. "I see you got my message."

"Yeah," Henry said. He pulled out a chair and sat. In public places, he always sat facing the entrance doorway, a carry-over from his youthful gang days when, at any given moment, the members of a rival gang might burst in and begin shooting.

"Maria," I said, "this is Henry Garavelli. Henry, Maria Hochs."

"Pleased to meet you," Henry said, and shook hands with her while glancing into the low-cut front of her dress. "What's up?" he said to me.

"The body's been returned," I said.

"Yeah?"

"Somebody dropped it off in a lot on Tyrone and Seventh."

"Mm," Henry said. "Any idea who done it?"

"None at all."

"Mm," Henry said. "So what does that mean? Is the case closed?"

"Yes."

"Mm," Henry said. "That's too bad, Ben, because it was beginning to get a little interesting."

"What do you mean?"

"Well, I been asking around ever since you were in the shop this morning, and I come up with some stuff that's got the boys on the street completely mystified."

"What kind of stuff?"

"Ben," he said, "do you know how many funeral parlors were busted into last night?"

"How many?"

"Four. And all down around Hennessy Street."

"Are you telling me four other corpses were stolen last night?"

"No, Ben. *Nothing* was ripped off. That's what's got the boys mystified. If somebody goes to all the trouble of breaking and entering, he's got to have *some* kind of crime in mind, don't he? And if he cracks a funeral parlor, he knows what to expect in there, right? He's going to find dead bodies in there and coffins and maybe some floral arrangements and a candlestick or two in the chapels. I mean, it ain't like he's going to find a television set and the family silver. So if a guy busts into a place like that and don't *take* anything, why'd he bust in to begin with?"

"How'd he do it, Henry?"

"Amateur night in Dixie. He forced the back doors with a crowbar."

"Have you got the names of the places he hit?"

"Yeah, I made a list for you. I figured you might be interested." He reached into his jacket pocket, pulled out first a bill from the electric company, and then a lined sheet of paper torn from a spiral notebook. He handed the sheet to me. On it he had carefully lettered the names and addresses of the four funeral parlors. I glanced quickly at the addresses. All of them were located within a rough twenty-block radius of the Gibson residence on Matthews Street. I folded the sheet again, and put it in my notebook.

"I still ain't got a line on the hoods who were muscling this Gibson," Henry said. "You want me to keep trying?"

"No," I said.

"So what do we do now?" Henry asked. "Just retire from the field?"

"I guess so," I said. "Our client's satisfied, Henry."

"Mm," Henry said. He looked suddenly disappointed. "Are *you* satisfied?" he asked.

"Not at all."

"Well," he said, "let me know if you need me again. Maybe when you think this over, you'll get some kind of inspiration. I figured at first we were maybe dealing with an international ring of body snatchers here. But there were stiffs in all those places, and whoever busted in didn't take so much as a fingernail. Well, who knows?" he said, and shrugged, and stood abruptly. "I got to get back to the shop."

"Henry," I said, "let me know how many hours you've put in on this, will you?"

"Yeah, yeah, no rush," he said. He glanced casually into the top of Maria's dress, said, "Nice meeting you, Miss Hochs," and walked away from the table. He still affected the cool, shuffling walk of a gang fighter, hands thrust deep into the pockets of his coveralls, shoulders slightly hunched, chin ducked. His eyes, which I couldn't see from behind, were undoubtedly covering every corner of the room as he walked toward the door, anticipating imminent attack. A good man, Henry.

"Is this too low-cut?" Maria asked abruptly.

9

I DROPPED Maria off at her apartment, and then drove three blocks west to one of the entrances to the road that ran through the park. As Henry had suggested, I began thinking over the information he'd given me, but I failed to come up with any sort of inspiration, brilliant or otherwise. The first possibility I examined was what I chose to call the Five Thief Theory, for lack of a better label. The Five Thief Theory worked on the premise that a thief driving a red-and-white Volkswagen bus had entered Abner's mortuary at three in the morning and stolen Anthony Gibson's corpse, while at different places within a twenty-block radius, four *other* thieves (working independently and without knowledge of each other or of the thief who'd stolen Gibson's body) were breaking into four separate funeral parlors from which they took nothing. Even though I knew the important role coincidence played in the resolution of seemingly baffling crimes, I dismissed this theory as too far-fetched.

It seemed to me that the five break-ins had to be linked. The thief had to have been looking for something he couldn't find in the first four funeral parlors, and only later found at Abner's. But if he'd been looking for something specific, and in this instance the something specific seemed to have been Anthony Gibson's embalmed body, then why had he later dropped it off in a vacant lot? It didn't make sense.

Without warning, something suddenly smashed into my windshield. My instant reaction was to duck away from what might become a deadly fusillade, cutting the wheel sharply at the same time, swerving up onto the grass bank beyond the shoulder of the road, and hurling myself flat on the front seat. Nothing else came. I waited a respectable three minutes and then lifted my head and peeked up at the windshield. The glass hadn't imploded, it hung in a spiderweb pattern to the metal frame. There was no bullet hole at the center of the web. Instead, there was a whitish powdery circle about three inches in diameter. Had someone thrown a rock at the car? I crawled across the front seat and opened the door opposite the wheel; if someone was gunning for me (even with rocks), he'd expect me to get out on the driver's side.

A crow was lying on the hood of the car.

He wasn't dead, but he certainly wasn't in the best of health after his recent collision with the windshield. His yellow beak kept opening and closing spasmodically, his wings and claws jerked as he fought unconsciousness. Birds do not appeal to me. I'd once written a letter to Alfred Hitchcock telling him so. Hitchcock never answered. I now debated what to do with this winged intruder who'd smashed my windshield and who now lay gasping for life on the hood of my car. Would my collision insurance cover the cost of a new windshield?

"How'd the accident happen, mister?"

"Well, a bird hit the windshield."

"A what?"

"A bird."

"Birds don't hit windshields, mister. Birds are very fast and very smart."

I looked down at the very dumb, slow bird. What was I supposed to do with him? Send him flowers and get-well cards? Feeling an enormous sense of guilt, I went back to the trunk, unlocked it, and located the cardboard carton containing flares, a flashlight, a set of highway tools, skid chains, and a box of cartridges for my .38 Detective's Special. I emptied the carton, went back to the front of the car, and gently eased the bird into it, figuring I'd leave bird and box safe and snug in the copse of trees lining the road. But suppose something in there decided to *eat* the damn bird before he was fully recovered? Swearing, I put the carton on the front seat and slammed the door. Then I went back to the trunk, took a wrench from the tool kit, came back to the front of the car, and broke out the windshield so I'd be able to see on the way home. The half-mile ride back to my apartment was breezy and cacophonous, the wind roaring in over the hood, the bird twitching and making croaking little sounds from inside the carton. He was still semi-conscious when I carried him into the apartment at twenty minutes to four. Lisette came out of the kitchen, drying her hands on a dishtowel.

Lisette Rabillon is my housekeeper, sixty-three years old, tall and slender, with sharp-nosed French features, shrewd blue eyes, and a saucy manner unbecoming to her age. A tough and beautiful old broad, she had fought with the French Resistance in her youth, earning the nickname "La Dynamiteuse," a testimony to her skill as a demolitions expert. In 1943 her husband had been taken as hostage when he refused to tell the names of the young Frenchmen who'd shot two German sentries. The commandant of the town ripped out his tongue and later stood him up against the wall of the church, where he was machine-gunned to death before the eyes of Lisette and the gathered townspeople. (I'm willing to forgive Lisette her sometimes dismal view of mankind.) She was living at present with a man who taught French at one of the city's universities, and who translated poetry and novels for a select few publishers. I had no reason to doubt that her relationship with the professor was hot-blooded and tempestuous.

She peered into the carton now, and said, *"Qu'est-ce que c'est?"*

"A crow," I said.

"Where did you get him?"

"He dropped in unexpectedly."

"Tell him to leave the same way," Lisette said.

"He's hurt."

"He'll die here and smell up the house."

"We'll see," I said, and carried bird and box into the back room while behind me Lisette mumbled something about "*des oiseaux sales.*"

The apartment I live in is eight rooms long, and the room I use as a study is at the farthest end, overlooking the park. Lisette doesn't much care for this arrangement because she has strict instructions never to let an unfamiliar stranger into the apartment, and this means she has to trot through the entire length of the place whenever she looks through the peephole in the front door and sees someone she doesn't know. There's only one large window in the room I use as a study. It's just opposite the door, and my desk is set at a right angle to it. The wall behind the desk and the one opposite it are covered floor to ceiling with bookcases and books. Very few of these books are novels (I despise novels), and *none* of them are mysteries (I abhor mysteries). When I'm sitting behind my desk, I'm facing one bookcase wall and another bookcase wall is behind me. The door is on my right, and the window is on my left and through the window I can see a magnificent view of the park and the buildings bordering it to the east.

I put the carton and the bird on one end of the desk now, and sat behind the desk and dialed Abner's funeral home. There was something I wanted to ask him, something triggered by the aimless woolgathering I'd done in the car before the crow decided to hit my windshield.

"Hello?" Abner said.

"Abner, it's Benjamin Smoke. Have you got a minute?"

"Certainly," he said.

"Is Mr. Gibson's body back in the shop?"

"Oh, yes," Abner said.

"Abner, is there anything wrong with the body?"

"Wrong?"

"Is there anything changed about it? Did anybody *do* anything to it, or *take* anything from it, or in any way *tamper* with it or *damage* it or . . ."

"No, Lieutenant. It's exactly as it was before it was stolen."

"I see," I said. "Thank you, Abner."

I hung up and stared at the telephone. Abner was no longer my client, his missing corpse had been found, the case was closed—but there was still no solution to it. If the thief had shopped four other funeral parlors before finding the corpse he wanted at Abner's, then why had he later discarded it in mint condition? In fact, why had he stolen it in the first place? I tried to find some joy in the knowledge that the theft had me completely baffled. In an attempt at self-deluding levity, I even told myself I could now go down to Abner's funeral home and make a citizen's arrest, charging him with violation of Section 1308 of the Penal Law: *"A person who buys or receives any property knowing the same to have been stolen . . . is guilty of a misdemeanor if such property be of the value of not more than a hundred dollars."* Anthony Gibson's corpse had become stolen property the moment the thief took it away in the dead of night. And Abner had received it this afternoon, and although the ninety-seven cents of elements in a human body had probably doubled or trebled with inflation, the stolen property was still worth much less than a C-note. You are guilty of a misdemeanor, Abner Boone, I thought, and tried to find some mirth in my observation. It didn't work. Until I knew exactly why four other funeral homes had been broken and entered, until I knew what had motivated the thief to settle upon Anthony Gibson's body and later discard it, I couldn't honestly say I'd expended every effort before admitting defeat. Which meant that I had to check out the mortuaries on the list Henry had given me.

I called Maria to tell her I'd probably be out for the rest of the afternoon and part of the evening, but if she'd like some company later on tonight, I'd be happy to oblige—provided nothing else developed. Maria said she'd be delighted to see me at any hour of the night or day, and just about then the bird in the box squawked and twitched.

"What's that noise?" Maria asked.

"A bird," I said.

"What do you mean?"

"I've got a crow."

"Yeah?" she said.

"Yeah."

"Male or female?"

"All birds are males," I said. "Especially crows."

"What's his name?"

"He hasn't got one."

"Oh, good, I'll think of one," Maria said.

"Don't bother. I'm letting him loose as soon as he's healthy."

"Is he sick?"

"He was in an automobile accident."

"Was he driving or just a passenger?" Maria asked.

"I don't find anything comical about this bird," I said.

"All right, grouch, call me later," she said.

"I will," I promised.

I put the receiver back onto its cradle and looked down at the bird. He was beginning to show some signs of life now, his eyes blinking, his black wings flapping weakly. I took a roll of masking tape from the bottom drawer of the desk and crisscrossed strips of it over the open top of the carton, just in case he came to and decided to fly all over the house while I was gone. Then I picked up the receiver again.

Through years of experience, I've learned that all garage mechanics are named Lou. Lou, the mechanic who usually serviced my car, first advised me that I ought to get rid of the heap, it was more trouble than it was worth, and it was also un-

American to own a foreign car. He then told me he'd have to turn the car over to a body and glass shop and they'd probably be able to put in a new windshield by the early part of next week, and the job would probably cost around two hundred dollars. I told him I'd drop the car off in just a little while, and then hung up and looked sourly at the blinking, flapping goddamn two-hundred-dollar bird. I went out into the kitchen then, drank a glass of cold milk, told Lisette I wouldn't be home for dinner, and left the apartment.

10

I TAXIED downtown from the garage to the first funeral parlor on Henry's list. It was much more sumptuous than Abner's modest establishment, with eight viewing rooms and two chapels, a managing director, an assistant director, and a staff of twelve, not including hearse and limousine drivers. The director was a moon-faced man named Hamilton Pierce. I identified myself as a city policeman investigating these mysterious break-ins, and then asked him how many bodies were on the premises at the time of his break-in last night.

"Four," he said.

"Embalmed?"

"All of them."

"Male or female?"

"Three women, one man."

"Can you describe the man to me?" I said.

"He's here now, if you'd like to take a look at him."

He accompanied me to one of the viewing rooms. A woman in black sat alone at the back of the room, facing the open coffin. She sat erect on a wooden folding chair in a row of identical chairs, her hands clasped in her lap. The room was filled with the overpowering aroma of the floral wreaths bedecking either end of the open coffin. I nodded respectfully to the woman in black, and then approached the coffin and peered into it. The dead man looked to be in his late sixties—it's sometimes difficult to tell with a corpse. He was perhaps five feet six inches tall, partially bald, a thick mustache over his upper lip. I estimated his weight to be about a hundred and fifty pounds. His hands were crossed over a Bible on his chest. His eyes, of course, were closed.

"What color are the eyes?" I whispered to Mr. Pierce.

"Blue, I believe."

"Had he been embalmed before the time of the break-in?"

"Yes."

I thanked Mr. Pierce for his time, jotted a description of the dead man into my notebook, and then hailed another taxi.

By six P.M. I'd hit all four mortuaries, and had compiled a list of the five male bodies the thief had passed up and the one male body he'd finally decided to steal. I automatically eliminated any of the dead *women* because I assumed the thief had been looking for a man's corpse; he had, after all, settled upon Anthony Gibson's. The page in my notebook looked like this:

	Corpse #1	Corpse #2	Corpse #3	Corpse #4	Corpse #5	Gibson
Age	68	58	19	37	45	42
Hair	Gray-Bald	Black	Black	Red	Brown	Brown
Eyes	Blue	Brown	Blue	Hazel	Brown	Brown
Height	5'6"	5'8"	6'2"	5'9"	5'7"	5'11"
Weight	150	145	190	170	160	185
Embalmed	yes	yes	yes	yes	yes	yes

The comparison list told me only that the thief had been looking for an embalmed male corpse, forty-two years old, with brown hair and brown eyes, measuring five feet eleven inches and weighing a hundred and eighty-five pounds. In short, the thief had been looking for Anthony Gibson—which brought me right back to square one. I suppressed an urge to giggle; big men look enormously foolish when they giggle, especially if they're standing on a street corner waiting for a taxicab. Instead, I tried to think like the thief.

I am the thief, I told myself, and I learn that Anthony Gibson has been killed in an automobile accident. *How* do I learn this? Well, in any number of ways. Despite the fact that Rhoda Gibson is not advertising it around, word of fatal accidents spreads very quickly. So let's assume that I—as the thief—hear about Gibson's death, and for some reason want his corpse. All right, I then assume the body will be taken to a mortuary somewhere in the vicinity of the Gibson residence, but I don't know which one. Then why don't I simply call the family of the deceased and ask where I can pay my respects? Well, perhaps I don't *know* the family of the deceased, in which case I couldn't possibly call to ask where the body will be laid out, especially if body snatching is on my mind. All right, so far so good. I draw a circle on a street map, using the Gibson residence on Matthews Street as the center of that circle, and I settle on an arbitrary radius of twenty blocks, figuring the body will be taken to a mortuary somewhere within that radius. I then look up the names and addresses of every funeral home inside my circle, and in the dead of night I begin searching for Anthony Gibson's body. I hit pay dirt on the fifth funeral home I break into. I take Gibson's body, and then . . .

Then *what?*

I *return* it!

Jesus, it didn't make sense, it *still* didn't make sense. I was back to zero again, I was stymied, I was beginning to feel a creeping sense of elation.

I decided to buy a present for the crow.

11

THE CAGE I bought was large and ugly, but I considered it only a temporary convenience for the bird, whom I expected to turn loose as soon as he was again able to cope with the perils of the city. I set the cage on the kitchen counter top, and then checked the bulletin board near the refrigerator. The note from Lisette was short and simple:

The bird is out. So am I!
Lisette.

Quickly, I went through the apartment to my study. The cardboard carton was still on the corner of the desk there, alongside the telephone. But the masking tape had been torn in several places, and the bird was nowhere in sight. I took off my jacket, pulled down my tie, and began searching the apartment.

I found him in the bedroom, perched on a lamp near the bed, shoulders hunched, beady eyes challenging, looking for all the world like a vulture.

"Come on, bird," I said pleasantly. "I bought a cage for you."

The bird did not answer.

"It's just until I can take you back to the park and let you loose."

The bird still said nothing.

"It cost me seven dollars," I said.

The bird uttered a distinctly threatening sound at that moment, and seemed ready to take off and fly directly into my face. I backed away toward the window. The bird was still crouched for flight, his beak opening and closing menacingly, his wing feathers bristling. He watched my progress across the room, and then stared at me intently as I opened the window.

"Get out," I said. "You want to roam loose in the city, that's fine with me. I was going to take you back where I found you, but no, you're just a hostile ingrate, so get out. Go on, what are you waiting for?"

The bird eyed me skeptically. Then, instead of flying to the open window, he took sudden wing from the bed and flew through the doorway into the corridor. I ran after him. He was in the living room when I caught up.

"You crap on my couch," I said, "and I'll shoot you dead on the spot." Instead of shooting him, I went out to the kitchen, took two slices of salami from the refrigerator, and tossed them into the cage. I carried the cage into the living room, placed it on the coffee table with the door open, and then moved away from it.

The bird suspected a trap.

"Go on, eat, you imbecile," I said.

The bird took three hopping, flapping steps across the couch, glared at me, poked his beak into the cage, glared at me again, and then entered the cage and began pecking at the nearest slice of salami. I bounded across the room and slammed the cage door shut. The bird flapped into the air, wings colliding against the sides of the cage, shrieking and yelling and hollering and making a terrible racket.

"As soon as my windshield is fixed," I said, "which *you* broke, I'm going to drive you over to the park and get rid of you. In the meantime, shut up and eat." The telephone rang. I looked at the bird once again, and then went into the study to answer it.

"Hello," I said, somewhat harshly.

"I've got a name for your bird," Maria said.

"I'm not interested," I said. "I'm taking him over to the park as soon as I get my car back."

"Where's your car?" Maria asked.

"Being repaired. It's a long story. Do you want to come here tonight, or shall I come there?"

"Is Lisette gone?"

"She's gone."

"I'll come there."

"Good," I said.

"It's a darling name," Maria said seductively.

"What is it?" I asked.

"Edgar Allan Crow," she said.

"Oh, boy," I said, and rolled my eyes toward the ceiling. But in my heart of hearts, I knew it was just the kind of cute, stupid, sickening name that would stick forever.

12

THE THING I liked best about Maria was that I never knew who she was going to be when we made love. She had come to me as innocently wide-eyed as a sixteen-year-old virgin, as lewdly inventive as a hundred-dollar hooker. I'd seen her slither from the bathroom like a houri in veils and pantaloons, heard her swearing beneath me in Spanish like a Barcelona gypsy. I'd watched her in garter belt, panties, and nylons (rarities in this abominable era of pantyhose) as she approached the bed, smelling of mimosa, breasts free, hair loose, eyes glittering. I'd seen her play the English governess, the rape victim, the match girl, the princess, and the secretary surprised. Maria Hochs was a crowd, and I never knew what to expect from her.

Tonight she was a nurse.

Tonight she was every erotic fantasy of a nurse any red-blooded American male had ever entertained upon entering a hospital. Her blond hair twisted into a tidy efficient bun at the back of her head, she came to the bed where I lay naked beneath the sheets. She was wearing a white slip, white dancer's tights, and white pumps. Sitting on the edge of the bed, she took my right wrist in her left hand, ostensibly to take my pulse, but before I quite knew what was happening, her free hand had slithered under the sheet. She kept calming me, reassuring me that the operation would turn out all right, urging me to relax while her restless hand urged otherwise. Excusing herself for just a moment, she took off the slip and came back to the bed wearing only brassiere, tights, and pumps. She apologized for having made herself so recklessly comfortable, but it *did* get so terribly hot in these hospital rooms, didn't I find it getting terribly hot in here? Reaching under the sheet again, she exclaimed that she felt sure I was developing a fever, and then suddenly threw back the sheet and widened her eyes in mock surprise, and smiled, and stood up, and backed away from the bed. The smile dropped from her face. Watching me, her gaze steady, she unclasped the bra and tossed it across the room, narrowly missing a chair near the dresser. Still watching me, she kicked off the pumps and then hooked her thumbs into the waistband of the tights, and eased them down over her hips and her belly, her thighs and her calves, and then stepped out of them with dainty abandon. She came to the bed again. Her hand went to the back of her head, her long blond hair fell loose. I held her close, and she murmured in my ear that everything was going to be all right, I had nothing to worry about, I would most certainly come through the operation—and the telephone rang.

I looked at the bedside clock. The time was twenty minutes to midnight. I lifted the receiver.

"Hello?" I said.

"Benny?"

"Is that you, Coop?"

"Yes," he said. "I didn't wake you, did I?"

"No, I was awake," I said, and glanced at Maria.

"I've got something I think might interest you."

"What is it?"

"About half an hour ago we caught a squeal from an old lady who was out walking her dog. She spotted a red-and-white VW bus parked behind a funeral parlor on Sixth and Stilson."

"Go ahead," I said. I was sitting upright in bed now.

"She got curious, went a little closer, and saw a guy carrying out a dead body. He put the stiff in the bus, and was just closing the door when the lady's dog began barking. She's got this little

Pekingese mutt, he started barking to beat the band. The car was parked under a light near the back entrance, so he must have figured the old lady got a good look at the plate—"

"Did she?"

"No, she's near-sighted, she wouldn't recognize her own mother unless she was standing a foot away. But *he* didn't know that, he must've figured he'd been spotted, and the car'd been spotted, so he came charging at the old lady with a crowbar in his hands. The dog started biting him on the leg, and the old lady took off one of her shoes and started hitting him and scratching him—she's some ballsy lady, I got to tell you. The guy was almost twice her size, but to hear her tell it, she almost flattened him. Windows are going up all around by now, so the guy panicked, dropped the crowbar, ran back to the bus, and drove off."

"Any prints on the crowbar?"

"The Detective Division and the lab boys are over there now. There's a lot more to this, Benny. It's pretty serious."

"Tell me."

"We dispatched an RMP car as soon as we caught the squeal. That was about a quarter to eleven. When the officers summoned entered the premises—"

"No cop talk, Coop."

"Sorry . . . They found a guy laying dead on the floor of the preparation room. That's where the bodies are embalmed, Benny. They call it the preparation room. Man had one of his own scalpels sticking in his chest. He's been identified as Peter Greer, one of the mortuary employees."

"Any blood on the table?"

"What table?"

"In the preparation room."

"I told you, the detectives are still there. I haven't seen any pictures or reports yet."

"Think they'd mind if I talked to the lady?"

"You'd better ask *them*," Coop said. "This is a homicide, you know."

"I know. Coop, thanks a lot."

"Don't mention it," he said.

I put the phone back onto its cradle.

"Something?" Maria said.

"Something," I said. "May I borrow your car?"

13

THE TWO DETECTIVES sent over from the Twelfth were Dave Horowitz and Danny O'Neil. I knew Horowitz, but I'd never worked with O'Neil before. In this city, the precinct detectives catching a homicide squeal are the ones who follow the case through to its hopefully successful conclusion. But the Homicide Division is notified nonetheless, and depending on the location of the crime, two men from either Upper or Lower Homicide arrive at the scene sometime after the investigating detectives have had a chance to do some preliminary work. The Upper and Lower are geographical determinations rather than qualitative judgments, the city being divided into halves where it concerns murder. The Homicide boys hadn't yet arrived by a quarter past midnight, when I reached the funeral parlor on Sixth and Stilson. Their absence wasn't keenly mourned. I had never got along with Homicide while I was on the force. In my estimation, Homicide cops are featherbedding duplicators, Players of a sort. Just outside the back door of the funeral parlor, I talked to Horowitz and O'Neil. The body of Peter Greer, the slain mortuary employee, had already been photographed and taken to the morgue for mandatory autopsy.

"Find anything out here besides the crowbar?" I asked.

"Just this," Horowitz said, and took an evidence envelope from his pocket and shook out a piece of jewelry onto a handkerchief in his other hand.

"What is it?" I asked. "Jade?"

"Looks like it."

"The old lady's?"

"No."

"You asked her?"

"We asked her," O'Neil said.

O'Neil was much younger than Horowitz and a lot less eager to cooperate with me. I could perfectly understand his probable line of reasoning. He was out here breaking his back for two hundred seventy-five dollars a week, and I was pulling down millions (ha!) with my private investigations. If he and Horowitz cracked this homicide, O'Neil wanted whatever was coming to him, without any of the glory going to a retired cop. He hadn't asked for my help or my hindrance, and he wasn't welcoming either now. Horowitz, on the other hand, was a man in his early fifties who'd been on the force long enough to realize he wasn't going to be Commissioner one day, nor even Chief of Detectives. He was a smart, hard-working Detective Second, and he knew how good (and modest) I was, and he knew that if I came up with anything that helped him to crack this, he and his partner would be the ones who got the commendations and/or promotions—not *me*.

"Can I get a better look at that?" I said.

"Sure," Horowitz said, and we moved closer to the light.

The pendant was oval-shaped, the jade set into a delicate silver frame that hung on a broken silver chain. The surface of the jade was carved with a bas-relief profile that looked Egyptian. Horowitz carefully turned the pendant over with one corner of the evidence envelope. The back of the pendant was silver, an extension of the frame into which the jade was set. The silver was engraved in delicate script lettering that read:

Natalie Fletcher

69 BC —

"Make anything of it?" I asked Horowitz.

"Not yet," he said.

"Any female corpses inside there?"

"Two of them," he said.

"I know just what you're thinking," O'Neil said. "Maybe this dropped off one of them when they were being carried in. You're wrong, Smoke. I already talked to the director here. The two lady stiffs are Janet Muehler and Sally D'Amiano."

"Did you get a name for the one that got away?"

"Huh?"

"The corpse that was stolen."

"Oh. Yeah," O'Neil said. "Guy named John Hiller."

"Age?" I said, and took out my notebook and was ready to start writing when I realized O'Neil wasn't about to start talking.

"Am I supposed to give him all this stuff?" he asked Horowitz.

"Why not?" Horowitz said, and shrugged rabinically.

"Suppose he fucks up the case?" O'Neil said.

"He won't," Horowitz said.

"He was thirty-seven years old," O'Neil said reluctantly.

"How tall?"

"Five-eleven."

"Weight?"

"A hun' eighty, a hun' ninety."

"Color of hair?"

"Brown."

"Eyes?"

"Brown."

"Any blood on the table in there?"

"No. Why?"

"I'm trying to find out whether or not Mr. Hiller had been embalmed."

"Then whyn't you just ask?" O'Neil said. "No, he was not embalmed yet. That's probably what Greer was about to do when the killer walked in on him. He was about to embalm the goddamn body."

"This old lady who tussled with the killer . . . did she give you a description of him?"

"All she said was he was big and husky."

"White or black?"

"White."

"What was he wearing?"

"Some kind of cap, leather jacket, she couldn't tell whether it was black or brown."

"What's *her* name?"

"I don't think we ought to tell him that, Dave," O'Neil said.

"Why not?" Horowitz said.

"It's one thing us talking to him, it's another he goes around questioning witnesses. We ever get this thing to court, I don't want the case thrown out because he was sticking his nose where it dint belong."

Horowitz shrugged again. "Maybe he's right, Ben."

"Okay," I said. "However you want it. It's your ball park."

A black unmarked sedan pulled to the curb. I knew before anyone got out of it that the boys from Lower Homicide were on the scene. Homicide boys seem to prefer black; it immediately announces their preoccupation. Both of them came into the alley, saw the shields pinned to the breasts of the topcoats O'Neil and Horowitz were wearing, and looked for identification on my coat. One of them asked who I was; I took out my shield and showed it to him. He was eagle-eyed enough to spot the minuscule blue-enameled "Retired" in parentheses under the "Detective-Lieutenant."

"That ain't worth shit," he said. "With that and thirty-five cents they'll let you in the subway."

"What are you doing here?" the other one said.

"He's a friend of mine," Horowitz said.

69

"Yeah?" the first one said. "Well, run along, friend. There's been a murder."

"Goodnight, gentlemen," I said, and walked out to the lighted sidewalk, and began looking for an open bar, or drugstore, or any place with a telephone directory.

14

I WASN'T OUT to get a beat on Horowitz and O'Neil, but I knew they'd be occupied at the scene for at least another hour, and by that time the Natalie Fletcher whose name had been engraved on the back of the pendant might have disappeared to Nome, Alaska. I knew, of course, that the pendant might have been dropped by anyone, and not necessarily by the man who'd stolen another corpse and killed a mortuary employee in the bargain. In fact, it seemed unlikely that the killer—described as a *man* by the old lady who'd struggled with him—would have been wearing a distinctively female piece of jewelry around his neck. But the chain *had* been broken, and the possibility existed that it had been torn from his neck while he and the old lady did their waltz and the dog nipped at his heels.

There was almost a full column of Fletchers in the phone book, but only one Natalie Fletcher. Her address was listed as 420 Oberlin Crescent, about two miles further uptown. I drove Maria's Pinto up Claridge Avenue, almost deserted at this hour of the morning, and reached Natalie Fletcher's building at one A.M., which is a very good time to question people, especially if they're murder suspects. I climbed three flights of stairs to the apartment indicated on the lobby mailbox. Outside her door, I put my ear to the wood and listened. Cops, retired or otherwise, *always* listen before knocking on a door. It's often difficult to understand conversations heard through layers of wood, but different voices *are* discernible and (provided everyone in the

room is speaking) the listening cop can get a pretty good idea of what's waiting for him behind a closed door. The only thing waiting behind Natalie Fletcher's door was silence.

There was no doorbell. I knocked. There was still no sound from within. I knocked again. It was a little after one in the morning, and if Natalie Fletcher was asleep, it might take a bit of banging to rustle her out of bed. I knocked again, louder this time. The door across the hall opened suddenly. I turned and found myself face to face with a tall, wide-shouldered man in his forties, his scalp shaved glistening clean like a stock company Yul Brynner's. His eyes were brown, overhung with shaggy blond brows. There was a Band-Aid taped to his right cheek, just below the eye. He was wearing a robe over his pajamas, his feet tucked into carpet slippers. Behind him in the apartment, I could hear the muted voices of actors in a late-night television movie.

"Are you looking for Natalie?" he asked.

"Yes," I said.

"She isn't here."

"Would you happen to know where she is?"

"No," he said. "Who are you?"

"Police officer," I said, and showed him my shield.

"Is she in trouble?" he asked.

"Are you a friend of hers?"

"I know her casually."

"What's your name?"

"Amos Wakefield."

"When did you see her last, Mr. Wakefield?"

"I don't keep track of her comings and goings," Wakefield said.

"Then how do you know she isn't here?"

"Well . . . I didn't hear any noise in the apartment when I got home tonight." He paused. "She's usually playing records."

"What time was that, Mr. Wakefield? When you got home tonight?"

"Oh, I don't know. Eleven-thirty, I would guess."

"Does she live here alone?"

"Yes."

"What kind of car does she drive?"

"What?" Wakefield said.

"Does she have a car?"

"I guess so. Why?"

"What kind of car?"

"I don't know."

"Would it be a VW bus?"

"No."

"You've seen the car?"

"Yes."

"But you don't know what year or make it is."

"It's some kind of station wagon."

"Mr. Wakefield, did you ever see Natalie Fletcher wearing a jade pendant with an Egyptian-looking face carved onto it?"

"No. What's this all about, anyway?"

"Just a routine investigation," I said.

"At one o'clock in the morning?"

"Well, we like to clear things up," I said. "Mr. Wakefield, would you happen to know whether Miss Fletcher's parents live in this city?"

"I know very little about her. We say hello to each other in the hallway, that's all."

"Then you wouldn't know any of her friends, either."

"No."

"Because, you see, if she isn't *here* at one in the morning, maybe she's spending the night someplace else."

"I wouldn't know."

"Or does she normally keep late hours?"

"I don't know."

"Well, thank you very much," I said. "I'm sorry if I woke you."

"I was watching television," Wakefield said.

"Cut yourself?" I said.

"What?"

"Your cheek," I said, and indicated the Band-Aid.

"Oh, that. Yes."

"Well, goodnight," I said.

"Goodnight," he said, and closed and locked the door. I went downstairs to the lobby and checked the mailboxes again. The superintendent's mailbox was the first in the row, marked simply SUPER. The apartment number engraved on the box was 1A, which I found on the ground floor, adjacent to the stairwell. The doorbell was similarly marked with a hand-lettered SUPER. I rang it and waited.

"Who is it?" a man asked from behind the door.

"Police," I answered.

"Police?" The door opened a crack, held by a night chain. I could see part of a grizzled chin through the crack, one suspicious blue eye, a corner of a mouth. "Let me see your badge," he said.

I held up my shield.

"Just a minute," he said, and closed the door again. I waited. Somewhere in the building, a toilet flushed. A baby cried briefly, and then was silent. On the street outside, I heard the raucous shriek of an ambulance. At last the door opened.

The super was a man in his sixties, a gray beard stubble on his face, his blue eyes heavy with sleep. He had thrown on a faded-green bathrobe over his underwear. His naked legs showed below the bottom of the robe.

"What is it?" he asked. "A burglary?"

"No," I said. "May I come in?"

"My wife's sleeping," he said.

"We'll be quiet."

"Well, okay," he said, "but we better be *very* quiet."

He stepped back to let me in, locked the door behind me, and then led me through the small foyer and into the kitchen. We sat at the kitchen table. From somewhere in the apartment, I heard someone snoring lightly.

"What's the trouble?" he said. His voice was hushed, there was the sense in that kitchen of two men who had risen early for a fishing trip.

"I'm looking for Natalie Fletcher," I said.

"Gone," he said.

"What do you mean?"

"Moved out."

"When?"

"Packed her stuff in the car Sunday night, drove off with it this morning."

"Did she leave a forwarding address?"

"Nope. Said she'd contact me about the furniture. Would you like a beer?"

"No, thanks."

"I think I'll have a beer," he said, and rose and padded to the refrigerator, and opened the door. "Shit," he said, "we're out of beer," and came back to the table.

"What about the furniture?" I said.

"Told me to try and sell it to whoever rented the apartment. Packed only her personal belongings in the station wagon."

"What kind of station wagon?"

"'71 Buick."

"The color?"

"Blue."

"Do you know the license number?"

"Nope."

"What kind of personal belongings did she pack?"

"Just clothes and like that. Three suitcases and a trunk. I helped her carry them down. She gave me five bucks."

"And this was Sunday night?"

"Yep."

"She packed the wagon Sunday night, but didn't actually get out of the apartment till this morning."

"That's right."

"You saw her when she left this morning?"

"Yep. Brought me the key."

"What time was that?"

"Nine o'clock."

"Did she leave the car on the street that night?"

"I wouldn't guess so, not packed with all that stuff in it. There's two garages right nearby. She must've left it at one or the other of them."

"How long had she been living here?"

"Moved in three months ago. In June, it was, the middle of June. What's she done? What's your name, anyway? Did you tell me your name?"

"Lieutenant Smoke. What's yours?"

"Stan Durski. What's she done?"

"What makes you think she's done anything?"

"Police lieutenant comes here in the middle of the night, I got to think she done something, don't I? Anyway, she's a crackpot. I wouldn't put nothing past her."

"How is she a crackpot?"

"She's crazy," Durski said.

"In what way?"

"She thinks she's Cleopatra. Do you believe in recarnation?"

"No, I don't."

"Me, neither. *She* does. You know what she thinks?"

"What does she think?"

"She thinks she's a recarnation of Cleopatra, how do you like that? She thinks she was born in the year 69 B.C. She used to tell me her father wasn't James Fletcher, he was Ptolemy the Eleventh—is that how you pronounce it? Ptolemy? And her brother Harry? The one died of a heart attack six months ago?"

"What about him?"

"He wasn't her brother. That is, he wasn't Harry Fletcher. You know who *he* was?"

"Who?"

"Ptolemy the Twelfth—is that how you pronounce it? Cleopatra married him when she was seventeen. He didn't die of a heart attack, Natalie said."

"How *did* he die?"

"He drowned in the Nile. You should see the way she dressed. I've got to tell you, she's a prime nut. She used to wear these long gowns, she copied them from pictures of Cleopatra at the museum. Hair was pitch-black, had it cut to just about *here*, just like Cleopatra. And sometimes she used to wear this cheap little crown on her head, and carry around a thing with a fake snake on it, that was supposed to be her scepter—is that how you pronounce it? Scepter? She had Cleopatra's make-up down pat, too, the eyes, you know, and the mouth. I got to tell you, she almost had me convinced sometimes. Do you know what she used to call my wife? My wife whose name is Rose Ann?"

"What did she call her?"

"Charmian—is that how you pronounce it? That was supposed to be Cleopatra's lady-in-waiting. I'm glad she's out of here, I've got to tell you. Now, if I can just sell all that crap she left behind . . . I told her, you know. I told her if I can't sell it to the new tenant, I'm just gonna throw it in the garbage. She used to call her living room 'the royal chamber,' you should see it. You never saw so much thrift-shop crap in your life. I was up there a couple of times, fixing something or other, there's always something going wrong in these old buildings. She used to keep the lights off all the time, she'd burn these candles, you know, I could hardly see what I was doing. And incense. Jesus, she used to stink up the whole building! And she'd play records with this eerie string music on them, and sometimes she'd talk to herself in what sounded like a foreign language—Egyptian, I guess it was. I don't know how to talk Egyptian, do you?"

"No, I don't."

"Oh, she's a crackpot, all right. It's a shame, too. She comes from a nice family."

"Are her parents still alive?"

"Both of them. I never met the father, though Natalie was always talking about him . . . Ptolemy the Eleventh, you know," Durski said, and rolled his eyes heavenward, and sighed. "Him and the mother are divorced. She's a nice lady, the mother. Stopped to talk to me whenever she came to visit and I was outside. We got along good, Violet and me. Violet, that's her name. Violet Fletcher."

"Where does she live?"

"Uptown someplace. On Fairmont, I think. I'm not sure."

"Mr. Durski," I said, "have you ever seen Natalie wearing a jade pendant with a—"

"Oh, sure, *all* the time. She told me it was a gift from her brother. Ptolemy. Said he hired the best sculptor in all Alexandria to carve her face on the jade. That's a crackpot, am I right?"

"The man across the hall from her . . ."

"Wakefield?"

"Yes. He said he'd never noticed her wearing it."

"Well, he keeps pretty much to himself. He probably *didn't* notice it."

"How long has *he* been living here?"

"Moved in about two months ago. What's Natalie done, anyway?"

"Nothing that we know of. We'd like to talk to her, that's all."

"Stan!" a woman yelled from somewhere in the apartment. "Is there somebody here with you?"

"No, Rose Ann," he yelled back. "I'm sitting here in the kitchen talking to myself."

"Stan?"

"Of *course* there's somebody here with me. There's a policeman here with me."

"Don't be so smart, Stan," she said.

"Mr. Durski . . . you mentioned that Natalie gave you her key when . . ."

"That's right."

"Do you still have it?"

"Yep."

"I wonder if I could have a look at the apartment."

"I don't see why not," he said. "You look like an honest man, and besides, there's nothing but a bunch of crap in there. I had a fire once in 7C, when the people was away, and the firemen came in and carried off everything that wasn't nailed down, they don't call them The Forty Thieves for nothing. And also, I get a lot of cops coming around here looking for violations so they can threaten me with a fine and get a payoff instead. But you look honest, and anyway, I'm gonna throw that crap in the garbage if I can't sell it to whoever rents the place. You want the key?"

"Would you like to come up with me?"

"Nope, I'd like to get back to sleep. Just drop the key in my mailbox when you're through, okay?"

"Stan!" his wife yelled. "Have you got the television on?"

15

I UNLOCKED Natalie's door without disturbing Amos Wakefield across the hall, eased the door shut behind me, and only then groped on the wall for a light switch. I found one to the left of the door.

A beaded curtain hung in the door frame of the small entrance foyer, separating it from the room beyond. The wallpaper in the foyer was white, with a boldly repeated palm-frond design in a green so dark it appeared black. I went through the curtain, found another light switch just inside the door frame, flicked it on, and was immediately transported back to a rather shabby ancient Egypt.

The palm-frond wallpaper continued into the room, its design less overpowering than it had been in the tiny foyer. Two *real* palms, both on the edge of imminent death, were against the wall opposite the beaded curtain. They flanked a huge wicker armchair sprayed with gold paint, undoubtedly Cleopatra's throne. A purple cushion was on the seat of the throne. Two cushions identical in size and shape, one blue, the other white, were on the floor before the throne. The wall behind the throne was hung with framed prints of the Pyramids, the Sphinx, a river I assumed to be the Nile, a frieze that looked as if it had been lifted from a dead Pharaoh's tomb, and a very lifelike drawing of a cobra. Two unfaded rectangles on the palm-frond wallpaper indicated where a pair of pictures had once been hanging. On the wall to the left of the throne, and at right angles to it, there was a closed door papered over with the palm-frond design, and sitting directly on the floor, either a mattress or a foam-rubber slab covered with a purple spread tucked in all around. I went to the door and opened it.

Unlike the shabby opulence of the royal chamber, the bedroom was spartanly furnished and looked almost severely modern in contrast. The walls were painted white, and there were no pictures on them, and no indication that any had been removed. A double bed was against the wall opposite the entrance door, beside a window overlooking an airshaft. There was a white shade on the window, flanked by hanging sheer curtains, also white. The bed was made up with sheets, pillowcases and a blanket, but no bedspread. A dresser finished in white enamel was opposite the bed, a cheap record player on top of it, a mirror over it. I went to the dresser. The drawers in it were empty except for the debris of packing—some bobby pins, an empty tube of lipstick, two pennies, and a ballpoint pen that must have cost twenty-nine cents when new. The single closet in the room was empty, too, except for some wire hangers on the pole and on the floor.

I went out to the foyer again, and then into the kitchen. The cabinets under the counters contained pots and pans, detergents, soap pads, some brown-paper bags, and a plastic trash container loaded with garbage. One of the hanging wall cabinets was stocked with perhaps a three-day supply of canned goods and standard grocery items. Another wall cabinet held six cups and saucers, eight dinner dishes, and half a dozen glasses. In a drawer beside the sink, there was what appeared to be a complete set of stainless-steel utensils, some paring knives, a bread knife, a can opener, a bottle opener, and a pair of serving spoons. The refrigerator was almost empty—a half-full carton of milk, a stick of butter (to which toast crumbs clung), a head of lettuce, an unopened container of blueberry yogurt, three slices of ham

wrapped in wax paper and sharing the meat tray with a shriv-
eled frankfurter. On a butcher-block cutting board beside the refrigerator, I found a fifth of Scotch with about three inches of
whiskey in it. There was no bulletin board or message pad near
the wall phone on the other side of the refrigerator, nor were
there any penciled numbers or messages on the wall itself. I
lifted the phone from its hook and got a dial tone; it had not yet
been disconnected.

I went back to the cabinet under the sink, took out the trash
container, opened one of the large brown-paper bags, sat on the
floor, and began sifting through Natalie Fletcher's garbage,
transferring it piece by sodden piece from plastic container to
paper bag. Garbage cans are often treasure troves to the working
policeman, but Natalie's garbage at first seemed to consist mostly
of orange rinds, coffee grounds, stale crusts of bread, empty soup
cans, soggy paper napkins, greasy paper toweling, cucumber and
potato peels, an envelope from the telephone company, an empty
frozen-juice can, more coffee grounds, and the crumpled comics
section of Sunday's newspaper. I kept looking. Toward the bottom of the container, I found some bills marked PAID, a dozen
cigarette butts undoubtedly emptied from an ashtray, an empty
beer bottle, a bottle cap, and a piece of a page torn from a calendar. I dug a little further and found three other pieces of the
same calendar page; she had obviously torn it in half, and then
in half again. I spread them out on the floor, and then put them
together like a jigsaw puzzle. September. This month's calendar.
Today was . . .

Until dawn came, it was still *today* and not *tomorrow* in my
mind—no matter how many hours past midnight it was. Today,
then, was still Monday, September 9. Natalie had moved out of
the apartment at nine this morning, but there was nothing on the
calendar to indicate that a move would take place today. This
seemed particularly strange, since the calendar page was a veri-

table appointment book for the month, with scribbles in most of the daily squares, penned or penciled reminders in what I assumed to be Natalie's hand:

September 3: *Hair, 3:00 p.m.*
September 5: *Bank, 11:00 a.m.*
September 7: *Dr. Hirsch, 1:15 p.m.*
September 8: *Call Mother*

The night of September 8 was the night five funeral homes had been broken into, the night Anthony Gibson's corpse had been stolen. September 9 was today; the square was blank. Beyond today:

September 10: *Susanna, 2:00 p.m.*
Mass, 12 Midnight

These last jottings seemed strange, too. Or, to be more exact, it seemed strange that I'd found them in with the garbage. If Natalie had intended to *keep* these appointments, why had she thrown away the calendared reminders of them? But on the other hand, if she *hadn't* intended to meet Susanna tomorrow at two o'clock, or go to church at midnight, why had she jotted them onto her calendar in the first place? I'd automatically concluded that Natalie was getting out of town; otherwise, why would she have left her furniture (such as it was) behind her, with instructions to sell it? But if she'd planned beforehand on leaving town, would she have made appointments in the city for tomorrow? Or had the move been a sudden decision? Or had she simply found a furnished apartment two blocks from here, moved her personal belongings into it, and left behind only the stuff Durski had accurately described as crap? I didn't know.

I put the brown-paper bag into the plastic trash container, swept up whatever garbage had found its way onto the linoleum, and then turned out all the lights and quietly let myself out of the apartment.

16

As Durski had promised, there were two garages in the immediate vicinity of Natalie's building. At the first one, the attendant had never heard of Natalie Fletcher or her blue Buick station wagon. I left and began walking up the street toward the second garage.

During the empty hours of the night, there are certain neighborhoods that take on the appearance of desolated, war-torn landscapes. The area in which Oberlin Crescent was located had once been a high-rent district, but that was back when you and I were young, Maggie. Even now, it had not yet succumbed entirely to urban blight, but it was well on the way, and all the signs of ultimate erosion were already there. The Crescent itself was perhaps one of a half-dozen oases in a desert of abandoned buildings, vacant and boarded-up stores, lots strewn with the rubble of torn-down buildings, unused vest-pocket parks with broken benches and graffiti-decorated walls and pavements, garages, a gasoline station, an all-night diner. In the empty lots, rats and wild dogs scavenged. In the abandoned buildings, derelicts squatted without water or electricity. The pavements were cluttered with empty wine bottles and newspaper scraps blown by the September wind. The river was only four blocks away, and I could hear the sound of a hooting tug, the rumble of trucks on the Harbor Highway. Up ahead, sitting on the front stoop of one of the abandoned buildings, three teenagers sat smoking. It was almost two o'clock in the morning.

They saw me approaching, and must have immediately sized me up as a cop. One of them got off the stoop. He stepped directly into my path, took a deep drag of the thin cigarette in his hand, and said, "You know what this is?"

"No, what is it?" I said.

"Grass," he said. "Are you a cop?"

I didn't answer him. He took another pull on the joint, and then giggled, and said, "Why don't you bust me? This is grass."

"We're not allowed to bust potheads after midnight," I said, and stepped around him and continued walking up the street.

"Hey, Officer!" he yelled after me. "Go fuck yourself!"

The second garage was on the corner of Dickens and Holt. The attendant was sitting in a small lighted office. He was reading a newspaper, his feet up on the desk, his transistor radio tuned to a rock station. Inside the garage proper, another man was hosing down an automobile. I hadn't intended to startle the man in the office, but the radio was up very loud and he probably didn't hear my approach.

"Excuse me," I said, and he swung around in the battered swivel chair, his legs coming off the desk, his eyes widening, the newspaper dropping from his hands.

"There's eighteen dollars in the cash drawer," he said immediately. "Take it."

"I'm a police officer," I said, and showed him my shield.

"Phew," he said. "You scared the shit out of me." He was a dark-skinned man with a narrow face, brown eyes, a thin mustache over his lip. He was wearing a yellow windbreaker over a garishly printed sports shirt, brown corduroy trousers, brown high-topped workman's shoes, white socks. He turned off the radio, and said, "What's up?"

"I'm trying to get a line on an automobile."

"Stolen?"

"No."

"What then?"

"I want to know if it was in here Sunday night."

"What kind of car?"

"A blue Buick station wagon."

"What year?"

"'71. It belongs to a woman named Natalie Fletcher."

"Oh, yeah. Cleo the Nut."

"You know her?"

"Everybody in the neighborhood knows her. She's a lunatic."

"Was the car here Sunday night?"

"It's here every night. This is where she parks it. Or *used* to park it, I mean. You can't leave a car on the street around here. They'll rip off the radio and the tires and the battery, they'll leave you with nothing but the shell."

"When you say she *used* to park it here . . ."

"Right, she moved away. Had three valises and a trunk in the car when she brought it in Sunday night. Gave me a fin to keep an eye on them."

"What time was that?"

"A little after midnight. I come on at eleven and quit at eight in the morning."

"What time did she come back for the car?"

"Around seven-thirty. Checked to see everything was still in it, and drove off."

"Did she say where she was going?"

"Nope. Just said she was moving out."

"Would you know the license number of the car?"

"I had it written on the tag with the extra set of keys," he said. "I threw the tag out when she picked up the car. The first part of it was 83L. That's how I remember the license plates, by the first three numbers or letters. That's how I write them on the board, like if somebody wants the car picked up or delivered. In this neighborhood, people don't like to go wandering too far from their houses. They give me a call, tell me they want the car brought over, I write down the first three numbers of the plate on the blackboard there, and Frankie—he's the one washing the cars outside—he drives it over, or picks it up, or whatever. Sometimes people get home late, they lock the car and leave it on the street outside their door, and give me a call when they get upstairs. We got duplicate sets of keys, so Frankie runs over and picks up the car and brings it here safe and sound. You be surprised how many people still live in this shitty neighborhood. How many cars you think we park here every night?"

"How many?"

"A hundred and twenty-two. That's pretty good, don't you think? I mean, for *this* shitty neighborhood? We got four Caddys, would you believe it? *Four* of them!"

"You wouldn't have thrown out that tag in the trash basket there, would you?"

"What tag?"

"The one with the license-plate number."

"Oh. Yeah, that's where I threw it. But I think that can's already been emptied."

"Would you mind if I checked it?"

"What do you mean?"

"Would it be all right if I went through that trash basket?"

"Sure, help yourself," he said. "It's 83L, that much I'm sure of."

"Are you through with that newspaper?" I said.

"I'm still reading it."

"I don't want to get your floor messed up."

"Try the barrel outside," he said. "Might be something there."

I went out into the garage and found a large barrel near the open door to the toilet. A copy of the city's tabloid newspaper was buried under a pile of greasy rags. I dug it out, carried it back to the office, and spread it on the floor. The radio was on again; rock-and-roll music blared from the speaker. The attendant ignored me as I went through the trash. He sat reading his newspaper and listening to the music. The trash here was not as messy as it had been in Natalie's apartment, but it was messy enough. When I reached the bottom of the basket, I became suddenly grateful for the mess. I had found no trace of the tag till then, and was ready to accept the fact that the basket had indeed been emptied sometime between nine o'clock this morning and now. But there was a sticky stain—syrup or oil—on the bottom of the basket, and stuck to it was a small white tag on a string. I plucked it out gingerly and looked at it. The ink was somewhat smeared from its contact with whatever viscous glop was on the bottom of the basket, but it was still clearly legible.

"This it?" I asked. "83L-4710?"

"That's it," the attendant said, without looking up from his newspaper.

"This wasn't an out-of-town plate, was it?"

"No, no."

I wrapped up the trash, put it back in the basket, thanked him for his time, and then went to the pay phone on the wall near the toilet. The door to the toilet was open, and the stench of stale urine wafted out to me as I dialed the Twelfth Precinct. It was my guess that Horowitz would be back in the squadroom by now, and would probably be up till dawn—this was a homicide. The desk sergeant put me through. Horowitz sounded very tired.

"Dave," I said, "I've got something for you."

"Yeah, Ben?"

"Natalie Fletcher, the name on the . . ."

"Yeah?"

"Her address was 420 Oberlin Crescent . . ."

"What do you mean *was?*"

"She moved out early this morning."

"Shit," Horowitz said. "I just sent O'Neil over there."

"Place is empty except for some junk," I said.

"You've been in there?"

"Yes, Dave."

"Ben, I don't think you should have done that."

"I knew you'd be busy at the scene for a while. I thought I'd save you some time."

"Where'd you get her address?"

"From the phone book. Same as you."

"Yeah," Horowitz said somewhat mournfully. "Well, is that it?"

"No, there's more. She left driving a '71 blue Buick station wagon, registration 83L dash 4710."

"This state?"

"Yes, Dave."

"That's good," Horowitz said, "I'll get on it right away." He paused, and then said, "I guess I owe you one."

"Did you find any prints on the pendant or the crowbar?" I asked immediately.

"Lab's checking them out now. I should have something by morning. What the hell time is it, anyway?"

"Quarter past two," I said.

"I feel like I've been up for a week," Horowitz said. "Anything else, Ben?"

"That's it. I'll keep in touch. Oh, one other thing, Dave. The lady's a bedbug. She thinks she's Cleopatra."

"How come I always get the fucking lunatics?" Horowitz said.

"Talk to you later," I said.

"So long," he said, and hung up.

I debated waiting till a more respectable hour before hitting Violet Fletcher, but time is of the essence in a homicide investigation. Out of courtesy, and because I didn't want to startle anyone's mother out of her wits by rapping on her door in the empty hours of the night, I looked up her number in the directory hanging from a chain on the wall, and then dialed it. She answered on the fifth ring. Her voice was fuzzy with sleep.

"Hello?" she said.

"Mrs. Fletcher?"

"Yes?"

"This is Lieutenant Smoke of the Police Department," I said. (A lie.) "I hope I didn't wake you, but a man's been killed, and I've been assigned to the investigation." (A partial lie.)

She was silent for a moment. When her voice came back on the line, she sounded decidedly awake. And decidedly skeptical. "What is this?" she asked. "A crank call?"

"No, Mrs. Fletcher, this is legitimate. If you'd like to call me back here at the squadroom, the number is Fieldstone 8-0765," I said, reading the number from the dial on the wall phone.

"Well . . . what do you want?" she said.

"I'd like to talk to you."

"So talk," she said.

"May I come there?"

"How do I know you're really a detective?"

"Mrs. Fletcher," I said, "I'll identify myself before you let me into the apartment. Or I'll stand in the hallway, if you prefer, and we can talk through the door."

"What did you say your name was?" she asked.

"Detective-Lieutenant Benjamin Smoke."

"What's that number again?"

"Fieldstone 8-0765."

"What precinct is that?"

"The Twelfth."

"I'll call you back," she said, and hung up.

In this city's telephone directories, an emergency number is listed for calls to the police, but the numbers of the individual precincts are listed as well. I was gambling now that Violet Fletcher, at 2:17 A.M., wasn't going to search through a phone book to verify the number I'd just given her. The phone rang not a minute later. I lifted the receiver from its hook and immediately clamped thumb and forefinger over my nose.

"Twelfth Precinct," I said, "Sergeant Knowles."

"Is there a Lieutenant Smoke there?" she asked.

"Yeah, lady, shall I ring?"

"Please," she said.

"Moment," I said, and released my nose, and let her wait a respectable forty seconds. Then, in my own voice, I said, "Twelfth Squad, Lieutenant Smoke."

"Yes," she said, "this is Violet Fletcher."

"Thank you for calling back, Mrs. Fletcher."

"You said someone's been killed."

"Yes. A man named Peter Greer."

"Does this have anything to do with my daughter?"

"Why? Does the man's name mean anything to you?"

"No. You haven't answered my question."

"It might," I said. "That's why I want to talk to you."

"When did you want to come here?"

"Immediately, if I may."

Mrs. Fletcher sighed. "I'll be expecting you," she said, and hung up.

17

I RANG the doorbell and waited. The peephole flap swung back.

"Yes?" a woman's voice said.

"Lieutenant Smoke," I said, and held my shield close to the peephole.

She studied it for what seemed an inordinately long time. Then she said, "All right," and unlocked the door, and slid off the night chain. The door opened wide. She looked me over, said, "Come in," and stepped back a pace. I went into the apartment, and she locked the door again, but she did not put on the night chain, presumably because she was in the presence of a policeman.

"I've made some coffee," she said. "Would you care for a cup?"

"Yes, thank you," I said.

She was a woman in her middle seventies. It was now two forty-five in the morning, and my phone call had undoubtedly awakened her, but she was attired as though for church, wearing a simple blue dress and low-heeled pumps, a string of pearls at her throat, her hair neatly coiffed, her face made up. She offered me a seat in the modestly furnished living room, and then went out to the kitchen. When she returned, she was carrying a tray with two cups of coffee, two spoons, a sugar bowl, and a creamer on it.

"I don't know how you take it," she said. "Please help yourself."

"I like it black," I said, and picked up one of the cups.

Mrs. Fletcher put two spoonfuls of sugar in her cup, and then added a dollop of milk to the mix. There was the creaking sound of footsteps in the apartment directly above. Pipes clanged somewhere next door.

"Is Natalie in trouble?" she asked.

"I don't know. May I ask you some questions?"

"That's why you're here," Mrs. Fletcher said, with the characteristic directness of intelligence seasoned with age. There's a nononsense air about smart old people. They've lived too long and seen too much, and they rarely bother with the niceties of polite conversation. They haven't got time for it.

"First I'd like to know if you've ever seen your daughter wearing a jade pendant."

"Why do you want to know that?"

"Because a jade pendant was found at the scene of the murder."

"And if I tell you my daughter *does* own such a pendant, will that implicate her in the murder?"

"Shall I be honest with you?"

"Why should I expect otherwise?"

"Mrs. Fletcher, if the pendant *is* your daughter's, I'd want to know how it got there. She may have a reasonable explanation."

"And if she hasn't?"

"First things first. *Is* it your daughter's?"

"Do you have the pendant with you?"

"No."

"Then how can I possibly identify it?"

"Does your daughter own a jade pendant mounted in a silver frame?"

"Yes."

"Is the face of it carved with a likeness of Cleopatra?"

"Yes."

"And is the back of the frame engraved with the name 'Natalie Fletcher,' and the date '69 B.C.'?"

"I have never seen the back of the pendant."

"Does the pendant I've just described to you sound like the one your daughter owns?"

"It does. But until I see the pendant, I can't say for sure it's hers."

"Mrs. Fletcher, this isn't a court of law, and I'm not trying to pin anything on your daughter. But a man's been killed . . ."

"Do you think my daughter killed him?"

"Not unless she can be described as big and husky."

"Natalie? You're joking."

"How tall *is* she, Mrs. Fletcher?"

"Five-six. But she's very slender. In fact, she's almost slight. I keep telling her she looks emaciated."

"Does she drive an automobile?"

"Yes."

"What kind of an automobile?"

"A Buick station wagon."

"Would any of her friends drive a Volkswagen bus?"

"I don't know any of her friends. What's more, I don't *care* to know any of them. They're probably to blame for . . . Well, never mind."

"Mrs. Fletcher, when did you last see your daughter?"

"What's today?" she asked.

"Technically, it's Tuesday morning already."

"Does that always confuse you, too?"

"Yes. To me, it's still Monday night."

"Let me think," she said. She sipped at her coffee. "I saw her Saturday. Yes. For a moment I wasn't sure whether it was Friday or Saturday. But it was Saturday. Yes. I remember clearly now. She had just come from the doctor's."

"Dr. Hirsch, would that be?"

"Yes," she said, surprised. "How did you know that?"

"Is Dr. Hirsch a psychiatrist?"

"No. He's an internist."

"Was your daughter sick?"

"No, it was just a checkup."

"And you met her afterwards?"

"Yes. We had lunch together."

"Was she wearing the pendant at the time?"

"She *always* wears the pendant. You see, she . . ."

"Yes, Mrs. Fletcher?"

"I don't know whether or not I can trust you, Mr. Smoke."

"Please do," I said.

Mrs. Fletcher sighed, put down her coffee cup, and then said, "My daughter thinks she's Cleopatra."

"I already know that."

"I assumed you did. When you asked if Dr. Hirsch was a psychiatrist . . ." Mrs. Fletcher sighed. "Natalie wears the pendant all the time, says it was a gift from . . ." She shook her head. "I can barely talk about it," she said. "I find it all quite sad."

"When did this start?" I asked. "The Cleopatra belief."

"Shortly after Harry died. My son. He died of a heart attack six months ago. Natalie said he couldn't be dead, people don't die, they just pass over into another life. Then she started saying he'd really died in the year 47 B.C., and then she said he was Ptolemy the Twelfth and she was Cleopatra and . . . and then she disappeared, I didn't know where she was living, I didn't know whether she was sick or . . ."

"When was this?"

"Harry died in March. March the fifth. Natalie left here in April sometime. I didn't know where she was until finally she called in June and told me she'd taken the apartment on Oberlin Crescent."

"You hadn't heard from her in all that time?"

"Not a word." Mrs. Fletcher's eyes turned suddenly angry. "I blame her friends. They're the ones who filled her head with evil ideas. Long *before* Harry died."

"Evil?"

"Yes. Spiritualism, witchcraft, the supernatural. *Evil*," she said flatly.

"Mrs. Fletcher, do you know where I can find your daughter now?"

"Have you tried her apartment?"

"Yes."

"She wasn't there, I suppose. I shouldn't be surprised. She runs around half the night to those masses of hers."

"Masses? What kind of masses?"

"Mr. Smoke," she said, "I don't want my daughter committed. I know she's under stress right now, and behaving strangely, but I keep thinking it's only temporary, she'll come out of it, it was just the shock of Harry's death. She loved her brother dearly, Mr. Smoke. There was a difference of only seven years in their ages—Harry was forty when he died, Natalie's thirty-three. They were always very close. I visit Natalie all the time now, I try to give her support, I keep hoping she'll come out of it. You must promise me that whatever I tell you, you won't try to have Natalie committed."

"I haven't the power to do that, anyway, Mrs. Fletcher."

"All right," she said. "Natalie's been attending black masses."

"Where?"

"I don't know. Somewhere in the basement of a church down-town. They invoke the devil. They make blood sacrifices."

Mrs. Fletcher fell silent. I waited. She was shaking her head again, staring into the coffee cup.

"I sometimes think, may God forgive," she said, "I sometimes think Harry's death was caused by witchcraft. Did one of Natalie's friends *do* something to cause the coronary? Did one of them put a curse on my son?"

"There's no such thing as witchcraft," I said.

"Isn't there?" she asked, and she raised her head, and her eyes met mine.

"No," I said firmly. "And there's no such thing as invoking the devil, either."

"I wish you'd tell that to my daughter," she said, and sighed.

"Mrs. Fletcher," I said, "do you have *any* idea where she might be?"

"None."

"Have you talked to her since Saturday?"

"I spoke to her on the phone last night."

"Sunday, do you mean?"

"Yes, Sunday. We're about to get mixed up again, aren't we?" she said.

"Not if we keep thinking of this as Monday night."

"Yes," she said. "This is Monday night, and she called me last night. Sunday."

"What did you talk about?"

"She seemed quite happy. She told me she was passing over into a new life. I hoped at the time—but I've been hoping this for a long time now—I hoped she meant she was finished with her Cleopatra delusion."

"*Is* that what she meant?"

"I don't know. She wouldn't explain. She said only that I might not hear from her for quite some time." Mrs. Fletcher frowned. "It was a very strange conversation, now that I think of it. Mr. Smoke, I'm suddenly frightened. You don't think she plans to harm herself, do you?"

"Has she seemed suicidal?"

"No. But . . . this business of . . . blood sacrifices, invoking the devil . . . I don't know. I'm frightened. I don't know what she's done, or may be about to do."

"Mrs. Fletcher," I said, "would you know anything about a midnight mass to take place tomorrow?"

"No, I'm sorry."

"Would it be one of your daughter's black masses?"

"I have no idea. It could be, I suppose."

"Does the name Susanna mean anything to you?"

"Yes. She's one of Natalie's friends. Susanna Martin. That isn't her real name. I don't know what her real name is. Susanna Martin is the name she uses. It's the name of a woman who was hanged for witchcraft in 1692."

"Do you know where she lives?"

"On Ninety-sixth, near Fairleigh. I don't know the address. It's a red-brick building with a green awning. I met Natalie up there one afternoon. We were going shopping, but she had to see Susanna first, and she asked me to meet her outside the building." Mrs. Fletcher looked directly into my eyes. "Are you going there now?" she asked.

"Yes."

"Be careful," she said. "Susanna Martin is an evil woman."

18

NINETY-SIXTH AND FAIRLEIGH was in Shrink City, where a plenitude of psychiatrists' offices nestled within a three-block area, bordered by the park on the west and Fairleigh Avenue on the east. To the north lay a Puerto Rican ghetto. To the south, Fairleigh and two other wide avenues plunged downtown to the heart of the city's business district. There was only one building with a green awning on Ninety-sixth. I stepped into the lobby and was walking toward the mailboxes when a doorman came briskly toward me.

"Hey, you!" he said. "What do you want here?"

"I'm a police officer," I said, and showed him the shield. "I'm looking for a woman named Susanna Martin."

"There's no Martins in the building," he said.

"Are there any Susannas in the building?"

"There's two *Susans*, but no Susannas," he said. "There's Susan Howell in 12C, and there's Susan Kahn in 8A."

"Let's try them both," I said.

"What do you mean *try* them? You mean ring the apartments?"

"Yes."

He looked at his watch and said, "It's three-thirty in the morning."

"I know that."

"Can't this wait till at least the sun comes up?"

"A man's been killed."

"I'm sorry to hear that," he said. "But if I go waking up a tenant in the middle of the night, I might lose a Christmas tip. Is the Police Department gonna make that up for me?"

"You can take your choice," I said. "Either ring them and tell them I'm here, or I'll go up and knock on their doors."

"You do that," he said. "I didn't even see you come in the building," he added, and turned his back and walked toward the switchboard in the corner of the lobby.

I took the elevator up to the eighth floor, found Apartment 8A, and rang the doorbell. A pair of chimes sounded inside. I waited, and then rang again.

"Who is it?" a man's voice said.

"Police," I said.

"What do you want?" he said.

"I'm looking for a woman named Susanna Martin."

"There's no Susanna Martin here," he said.

"Is there a Susan Kahn?"

"Yes, she's my wife."

"Would you mind opening the door, sir?" I said.

"Mister," he said, "if you told me you were the mayor himself, I wouldn't open the door for you at this hour of the night."

"How about just opening the peephole and looking at my shield?"

I heard the peephole flap being thrown back. I held up the shield.

"Very nice," he said. "If you've got legitimate business here, go get a warrant."

"Mr. Kahn," I said, "would your wife happen to know someone named Natalie Fletcher?"

"No," he said. I heard the final click of the peephole flap. "Goodnight," he said.

I went back to the elevator and rode it up to the twelfth floor. Outside 12C, I looked at the nameplate—SUSAN HOWELL—and rang the doorbell, and waited. This time a peephole flap went up before anyone said anything. I stood well back from the door to give whoever was studying me a full-length picture.

"What is it?" a woman's voice said.

"I'm looking for Natalie Fletcher."

"She's not here."

"Do you know her?"

"I know her. She's not here."

"May I come in, please?"

"Do you know what time it is?"

"Yes."

"Come back later," she said.

"I'm a police officer," I said, and held up my shield.

There was a silence. Then she said, "Just a moment, let me put something on."

It took her five minutes to put something on. When she came back to the door, she opened it only a crack, a night chain tethering it. "Let me see that badge again," she said. I held it up to the crack. "It says 'Retired,'" she said.

"That's right."

"I don't have to let you in here," she said.

"Natalie's in trouble."

"What kind of trouble?"

"Miss Howell, we'll wake up the whole building."

"I don't care about the whole building. What kind of trouble is Natalie in?"

"Do you know where she is?"

"Answer me first."

"She's wanted for questioning."

"About what?"

"A murder. Miss Howell, would you please open the door?"

The night chain came off, the door opened wide.

Susan Howell was a woman in her late thirties. She was wearing a white quilted robe over a long pink nightgown. Her hair was carrot-colored and frizzy, standing out from her narrow face like the coiffure created for the bride of Frankenstein's monster. Her nose was thin and long, ending in a contradictory tip-tilt. She had pale-amber eyes, like a cat's, and she studied me for a long moment before she said, "Come in." She was perhaps five feet seven inches tall, and her carriage was ramrod stiff. As I moved past her, I felt somehow very short. She closed and locked the door behind me, and then said, "In there."

I walked into a living room illuminated by a single lamp on an end table. The walls were painted black. I had never before been in a living room with black walls.

"Sit down," she said.

I sat in a black-leather armchair. The other furniture in the living room was black, too. I had the feeling I was sitting in the dark, even though the lamp threw plenty of light into the small room. Susan Howell sat opposite me in a wing chair upholstered in black brocade.

"What's this about Natalie?" she asked.

"I told you. She's wanted for questioning."

"The police want to question her?"

"Yes."

"But you're not a policeman."

"I'm a retired policeman."

"Are you asking me to believe that the police would send a retired cop to investigate a murder?"

"It's not unusual. I've had years of experience. The department often calls me for advice and consultation." This was an outright lie. In the four years since I'd retired, the Police Department had never so much as sent me a Christmas card.

"I don't believe you," she said.

"The man in charge of the case is named Dave Horowitz," I said. "He's a second-grade detective on the Twelfth Squad. Call him. He'll tell you I'm here on behalf of the police."

She considered this for several moments. Neither of us spoke. Someplace in the apartment, a clock ticked noisily. At last she sighed, and said, "I'll answer your questions. But first I want to know who was killed."

"A man named Peter Greer. He worked at a funeral parlor. He was about to embalm a corpse when somebody stabbed him. Tell me, Miss Howell, would you happen to know where Natalie Fletcher is?"

"I have no idea where she is."

"When's the last time you saw her?"

"A month ago."

"Are you expecting her tomorrow?"

"No."

"Have you spoken to her on the telephone since you last saw her?"

"No."

"Then how do you know she isn't home?" I said.

"What?"

"You told me you don't know where she is. How do you know she isn't at 420 Oberlin Crescent?"

"I . . . I assumed you'd already been there."

"Why'd you assume that?"

"It's what a policeman would do."

"Miss Howell," I said, "would you—?"

"I prefer that you address me by my proper name," she said, suddenly.

"And what's that?"

"Susanna Martin," she said, and added immediately, "The witch of Amesbury."

"All right, Miss Martin, is it true that Natalie Fletcher has been attending black masses at which blood sacrifices are made?"

She suddenly burst out laughing.

"What are you laughing at?" I asked.

"Well may I laugh at such folly," she said. Her voice sounded different. Not only had her language changed abruptly, but so had her normal speaking voice.

"Do you know that Natalie has been attending black masses?"

"I don't desire to spend my judgment on it," she said. "If she be dealing with the black arts, you may know as well as I."

"Her mother . . ."

"A curse on mothers!" she said. "Was not Sarah Atkinson of Newbury a mother? And did she not, when I was sorely taken with the witchcraft, report to the magistrates that I had once in weather foul walked to her home from Amesbury and entered her kitchen with the soles of my feet dry? And when she said to me, 'I'd be wet to my knees if I'd come so far,' was I not right to reply, 'I scorn to have a drabbled tail?' A curse on all mothers, a curse on the goodwife who saw me melt into nothingness and then reappear in the form of pecking, pinching birds. And a curse on fathers, too, and on thee, and on thine own father! A curse on John Kembal, to whom I sent the vanishing puppies, as black they were as the heart of Jesus, to leap at his throat and his belly, immune to his swinging ax! 'In the name of Jesus Christ avoid!' he shouted, and the puppies relented, but though I gave him puppies enough, I curse him still."

"Miss Martin," I said, "why is Natalie coming here tomorrow?"

"To hear me tell of Tituba the slave, half-black, half-Carib, and of the tricks and spells and voodoo magic she brought from the Barbados to Salem Village."

"I don't think she'll be here," I said. "She's moved out of the apartment on Oberlin Crescent. The place is empty."

"Thy head is empty," she said.

"Her mother spoke to her last night. Natalie told her she was passing over into a new life. Do you have any idea what that might have meant?"

"It is a shameful thing that you should mind these folks that are out of their wits."

"Do you know where Natalie's gone?"

"I would say if I knew. I do not know. Look!" she shouted, and pointed toward the ceiling. "There sits Goody Cory on the beam, suckling a yellow bird betwixt her fingers."

I looked up. There was nothing on the ceiling.

"Don't you hear the drumbeat?" she asked. "Why don't you go? Why don't you go?"

"*Where?* Where can I find Natalie?"

"There stands Alden," she said. "A bold fellow with his hat on before the judges. He sells powder and shot to the Indians and French, and lies with Indian squaws and has Indian papooses."

"Is Alden someone Natalie knows?"

"Ask John Indian," she said.

I didn't know whether John Indian was real or imagined, but I knew there was no point in asking Susan Howell *or* Susanna Martin any further questions. I'd put her on guard back there when I'd asked how she knew Natalie was not in the Oberlin Crescent apartment; it was then that she'd gone into her Salem Village routine. True delusion or diversionary tactic, there was no getting her out of it now.

"Well," I said, "thanks a lot. I won't take up any more of your time."

"When did I hurt thee?" she asked, and grinned.

I walked to the door.

"No further questions?" she asked.

"None," I said.

"No more weight?" she said, and grinned again.

I went out of the apartment. She closed and locked the door behind me. I pressed my ear to the wood. If she was making a hurried telephone call, I could not hear her dialing. I walked to the elevator and rang for it. I didn't know much about the history of witchcraft in Salem, but I did know that when Giles Cory, an accused witch, was being pressed to death in an open field next door to the jailhouse, rock upon rock being piled upon his chest in an effort to get him to confess to the crime of witchcraft, he had maintained silence almost to the end. And then he had said only, "More weight."

19

It was beginning to look very good.

The killer had made only one mistake that I could see, the very mistake that had transformed him from a body snatcher into a murderer. He should not have slain Peter Greer, the mortuary attendant. Up to that moment, his crime had been strictly small-time stuff, punishable by a nickel stretch in jail or a thousand-dollar fine, or both. But his need for a corpse had been so overriding that he'd committed the biggest felony of them all, and that had been a blunder.

But aside from that (and I had to consider his attack on the dog-walking old lady a simple extension of the homicide), he had made no other mistakes, and I still didn't know why he'd wanted a dead body, or what he planned to do with it. Yes, I *had* considered the possibility that the "mass" marked on Natalie's calendar was to be a witches' Sabbath requiring a blood sacrifice from a fresh corpse—the killer had, after all, returned a corpse already drained of blood, and stolen one that hadn't yet been embalmed. But blood sacrifices were usually *living* victims, a goat or a lamb or—in some cultures—a human being brought to the altar and held there while its throat was slit, its blood allowed to drip into a sacrificial basin. A *dead* offering? As a *blood* sacrifice? The two concepts seemed contradictory and mutually exclusive. Besides, assuming someone had been after a warm body (so to speak) for later use in a blood sacrifice, would he have *killed* someone while stealing that body? There's nothing in the Penal Law that makes it a crime for criminals to behave illogically. But if the possibility of murder had even peripherally occurred to the body snatcher, why hadn't he simply snatched a *live* body, and committed his murder on the altar, as a *genuine* blood sacrifice? No, I didn't think the swiped body was intended as an offering at a mass—black or otherwise. Then why *had* it been stolen?

I was whistling as I went into the apartment. The sun wasn't up yet, nor was there yet a hint of dawn in the sky. I flicked on the kitchen light, and the crow in his cage cawed in what I assumed was annoyance rather than greeting.

"Hello, stupid," I said, "did anyone feed you?"

The bird squawked again.

I looked into his cage. Not a scrap of food was anywhere in sight. I went to the refrigerator, discovered that the meat tray was empty, and found an open can of tuna fish on one of the shelves. Operating on the theory that crows—like sharks—will eat *any* kind of crap, I spooned the contents of the can into the cage. The crow regarded it suspiciously. I closed the cage door and looked at the bulletin board. No calls. Loosening my tie, I went into the study and dialed the Twelfth Precinct. Dave Horowitz was still there.

"Yes, Ben?" he said.

"Anything from the lab yet?"

"At five in the morning?" he said. "What the hell's the matter with you?"

"What's the matter with *you*, Dave?"

"Nothing." He paused. "Well, yes, something. I'm getting a lot of static from my partner. He doesn't like you nosing around on this."

"I'm saving him legwork, Dave."

"Well, he doesn't look at it that way."

"How does he look at it?"

"He says you're running the goddamn case for us."

"I'm not doing that at all."

"I'll tell you the truth, Ben, *I'm* a little nervous, too. This is a homicide. If we crack it, I don't want it fucked up in court."

"That's just what your partner said."

"Well, maybe he's right. This is a *job* for us, Ben, and for you . . ." He paused. "Well, forget it."

"No, go ahead."

"Well, O'Neil thinks this is only like a hobby for you."

"It's not a hobby, Dave."

"I'm only telling you what he thinks."

"So I guess when you *do* get that lab report . . ."

"Come on, Ben, don't make me out a heel. I got one too many ulcers as it is."

"Do *you* want me to lay off?"

"I don't know what I want. That stuff you gave me on the car was real meat. Maybe O'Neil *wouldn't* have come up with it, who knows? At the same time, I don't want you to do anything that'll maybe blow this thing in court, you follow me?"

"Give me a little more credit than that, Dave."

"Ah, shit, Ben," he said, and fell silent. I waited. He was thinking it over. I gave him plenty of time. He sighed, and then said, "I ran an I.S. check on Natalie Fletcher. She hasn't got a record, but there was a cross-reference card on her." I waited some more. He was still struggling with it, and I liked him too much to push him. "You'll be careful, huh, Ben?" he said at last. "I can get my ass in a sling on this."

"I'll be careful."

"The blue card fed back to one Charles S. Carruthers. He's got a yellow sheet as long as my arm, starting from when he was fifteen. Last time out, he got busted for Burglary One, drew the maximum, got paroled last October after serving twelve and a little more."

"What's the connection between him and Natalie?"

"According to his parole officer, they're living together."

"As of when?"

"As of the P.O.'s last report. I've got the date here, just a second." There was a long pause on the line. "August fifteenth."

"Have you got an address for him?"

"Yeah, and it's not Oberlin Crescent."

"What is it?"

"8212 McKenzie. I can only figure she was living one place and sleeping another."

"Have you talked to Carruthers yet?"

"O'Neil should be up there right this minute."

"8212 McKenzie. That's in Hammerlock, isn't it?"

"That's where it is."

"Is Carruthers black?"

"He's black."

"What else have you got on him?"

"Thirty-six years old, six feet two inches tall, weight a hundred ninety. Brown eyes, black hair, knife scar on his right wrist, no other identifying marks or tattoos."

"That burglary fall? Was it the heaviest on his sheet?"

"Depends how you look at it. When he was seventeen a pusher allegedly sold him some bum shit, and he took off after the guy in an automobile, ran him down, and killed him. He was charged with Homicide Two, reduced to Manslaughter One, reduced again to Criminal Negligence, Vehicular. He was sentenced to five, served two and a half."

"Has he been clean since he got out on the burglary rap?"

"One warning from his parole officer."

"For what?"

"The P.O. got an anonymous call from a guy who said Carruthers had been at some kind of meeting where everybody was wearing masks. So he warned Carruthers that such assemblages were violations of Section 710. You know the section?"

"I know it."

"It's a bullshit section. Anyway, Carruthers claimed he'd never been to any such meeting, so that was that."

"What kind of meeting was it?"

"Well, it couldn't have been a legitimate masquerade party or fancy-dress ball, because the section excludes those."

"Could it have been a black mass?"

"What do you mean? Colored people in a church?"

"No. A witches' Sabbath."

"Ben . . . I'm very tired, I've been up all night. Don't clown around."

"Okay," I said. "Thanks a lot, Dave."

"Yeah," he said, and hung up.

I was suddenly exhausted. I put the receiver back on the cradle, and then went out of the study and into the bedroom. Maria was asleep, the sheet tangled around her legs, her long blond hair spread on the pillow. I took off my clothes, got into my pajamas, and crawled into bed beside her.

"Ben?" she said.

"Yes."

"Good," she said, and rolled in against me.

20

THERE WAS sunlight in the room; it was Tuesday morning at last. On Maria's pillow I found a note that read:

Dear Ben,
I have a ten o'clock reading, and besides, I don't like Lisette to know I sleep with you. I'm not sure whether you'll need the car again today, and anyway, I don't know where you parked it. So I'll take a Taxi. Will you call me later? I'll leave a message with my service. Love you. Be careful.
Maria
P.S. I have fed Edgar Allan.

I looked at the clock. It was twenty minutes after one. I hadn't intended to sleep so late. I put on a robe (for some undoubtedly perverse reason, I don't like to talk to anyone on the telephone when all I'm wearing is pajamas), went into the study, and dialed the Twelfth Precinct. The desk sergeant told me Horowitz had gone home. I asked him to put me through to Coop's office instead.

"Good afternoon, Benny," Coop said. He sounded very official and a trifle brusque.

"Coop," I said, "I hate to bother you with this, but Dave Horowitz was waiting for a lab report . . ."

"I have it here on my desk," Coop said. "Benny, I've got a very unhappy cop upstairs in the squadroom, and even though I love you like a brother, I've got to keep the detective team working togther as a functioning unit of this precinct. You understand me?"

"What the hell is O'Neil worried about?"

"I'll tell you what he's worried about, if you'd like to know. Last night he gets to Natalie Fletcher's apartment, and you've already been there. He talks to the super, you've already talked to the super. The super tells him the mother's name, and this morning O'Neil goes to see her, and finds out you were there in the middle of the night, and what's more you were leaving there to talk to somebody named Susanna Martin. Who's Susanna Martin, Benny? O'Neil went up to that building on Ninety-sixth and couldn't find anybody by that name."

"Tell him to keep trying, Coop. He's such a hotshot . . ."

"He's a good cop, and I don't like to see him upset."

"What's in the lab report, Coop?"

"No comment."

"How about the VW bus? Anything on that yet?"

"Benny, you are not going to get anything further from me," Coop said, and hung up.

I sat at the desk for a moment, trying to work out my next move. There had undoubtedly been something positive in the lab report. Otherwise, it would have been simpler for Coop to have said, "Sorry, nothing. No latents." I decided to call the lab direct. I knew the number by heart, I had dialed it all too often in my years on the force. The assistant who answered the phone wanted to know who I was and why I wanted to talk to Detective-Lieutenant Ambrosiano. I told him my name, and said it was a personal call. He said the lieutenant's line was busy, and I'd have to wait. I waited. In the kitchen, I could hear the crow squawking at the top of his lungs.

Michael J. Ambrosiano was the man in charge of the Police

Laboratory downtown in the Washington Plaza complex, where the new Police Headquarters building was located. His lab occupied all of the ninth floor and part of the tenth in the huge thirty-four-story structure which, from the outside, seemed to have been constructed entirely of glass. So many windows were unusual for a building housing policemen of every stripe and color. The windows in any precinct, for example, are usually covered on the outside with a heavy-gauge wire-mesh grille, it not being uncommon for cop lovers to toss rocks or stink bombs into the place. Not so at Headquarters, which housed the Lab as well as the Identification Section and the Property Clerk's office (from which a million dollars' worth of confiscated heroin had been stolen only last year, the less said about that the better), and the offices of the Police Commissioner and his Deputy Commissioners, the Chief Inspector, and the Chiefs of Patrol, and Detectives, and Personnel, and the offices of Personnel Records (Civilian and Uniform), and the office of the Employees Relations Unit, and the Press and Public Relations office.

Mike Ambrosiano was a policeman and a scientist both, a man of sensitivity and skill who had, while I was a working cop, helped me on more occasions than I could count. He was forty-six years old, with blond hair going slightly gray, and blue eyes that weighed with equal scrutiny a laundry mark inside a dirty shirt or a trace of poison in a coffee cup. We had worked well together over the years, and I felt I could now ask him for a favor without compromising either his professionalism or his integrity. I was mistaken.

When he came onto the line, he said, "Coop just called. That's who I was talking to."

"Oh," I said.

"Mm," Mike said. "He figured you'd be trying me next."

"So I guess the answer is no."

"I'm sorry," he said. He sounded genuinely sorry.

"Must be something pretty hot in that report."

"I haven't even seen it," Mike said. "Ryan handled it."

"You don't suppose Ryan would like to tell me about it, do you?"

"I doubt it. Ryan is a very secretive type."

"I figured he might be."

"Ben, why don't you let this go?" Mike advised gently. "Getting back the kraut's jewels was one thing. But this is homicide."

"I can't let it go," I said. "I'm possessed."

"Did you hear the one about the lawyer who took on an exorcist as a client?" Mike said, and began chuckling immediately.

"Tell me," I said.

"Well, this exorcist came to a lawyer complaining that he'd done some work for a man who'd been possessed, you know? Got rid of the devil inside him, all that stuff."

"Yeah?"

"But the guy who'd been possessed refused to pay the exorcist for his services. So now the exorcist wanted satisfaction. So the lawyer called the guy and said he was representing the exorcist, and unless the guy paid the money he owed, he'd see to it that he was repossessed." Mike burst out laughing. I smiled.

"Mike," I said, "did you find any latents on either the crowbar or the pendant?"

"Ben," he said, "it's always good talking to you, give me a ring again sometime, huh? Maybe we can have lunch."

I heard a click on the line. He had hung up. In the kitchen, the bird was yapping madly. I depressed one of the buttons on the receiver rest, got a dial tone, and immediately phoned Henry Garavelli. He picked up on the third ring.

"Garavelli Television," he said.

"Henry, this is Ben. Are you free this afternoon?"

"What's up?" he said.

"I'm looking for a lady named Natalie Fletcher," I said. "Thirty-three years old, five feet six inches tall, slender, long black hair, may be dressed as Cleopatra."

"Cleopatra?"

"That's right, Henry. I'm expecting her to show at 12 East Ninety-sixth, near Fairleigh. She's supposed to visit a woman named Susan Howell at two o'clock, Apartment 12C. If she shows, she may be driving a 1971 blue Buick station wagon. Stick with her, and get back to me."

"Got you," he said, and hung up.

I went out to the kitchen, and told the bird to shut up. He did not shut up. He yammered all the while I prepared myself some bacon, eggs, toast, and coffee, and continued squawking while I ate. I put the dishes into the sink, glared at the bird before I left the kitchen, and then showered, shaved, and dressed for the trip uptown to Hammerlock. I was just leaving the apartment when Lisette let herself in with her key. It was five minutes to three, and she usually came to work at eleven in the morning. Lisette had a hangover. She explained that René Pierre, her professor friend, had brought home a case of very good Bordeaux last night, and they had consumed three bottles of it before midnight.

I told her to go swallow a raw egg.

21

THERE ARE almost eight million people living in this city, and nine percent of them—more than 700,000—are black. Of these, close to half a million live in the rank ghetto known as Hammerlock. Knowing the bitter humor with which slum dwellers baptize the rat-infested areas in which they're forced to live (as, for example, *La Perla* in San Juan, a pearl indeed), you might automatically conclude that the name of a wrestler's hold had been applied to Hammerlock only *after* it became a slum—the grip of poverty metaphorically pulling the slum dweller's dignity up behind his back and yanking on it till it broke.

Wrong.

Once upon a time, and long before my own Dutch grandfather came to these shores, the section now known as Hammerlock was interlaced with canals built by his ancestors. The harbor and river, then as now, were busy with seagoing traffic; the network of canals eased the clutter, diverting barges loaded with merchandise onto the inland waterways. Hammerlock in those days was an area of farms and forests, its dirt roadways permitting the passage of a single horse and wagon, or a coach perhaps, but certainly not two of them approaching from opposite directions. The canals were speedier and safer; then, as now, there were highway robbers everywhere, and they probably thought twice before sticking up a barge, which was a crime close to piracy on the high seas and punishable by hanging. In any case, as with all

canal systems, there were locks. These locks were named after
the keepers who ran out of the canalside shacks to open the gates
whenever a barge approached. Buersken's Sluis, Goedkoop's
Sluis, Favejee's Sluis, Weidinger's Sluis were all part of the system. As was Hemmer's Sluis. Well, when the roads were im-
proved, the canals were filled in (some of them, in fact, were
filled in to make roadbeds), and the names of the locks vanished
together with the locks themselves and the canalside shacks that
had dotted the landscape. But the keeper Hemmer had constructed for himself a house of huge stones cleared from the field
beyond his lock, and this remained on the site long after the
canal running past it had been filled in. The house itself became
known as Hemmer's Sluis, which was changed to Hammer's Lock
when the English took over the city, and later, long after the
house itself had been burned down by the Hessians fighting
Washington's troops, this was shortened to Hammerlock. As a
matter of interest, the northernmost corner of the slum named
Hammerlock—the part that jutted into the river and pointed a
jagged finger of land toward the next state—was called Land-
slook, a bastardization of Lange's Lock from days of yore.

I got uptown at about ten minutes to three, found a garage on
Liberty and 104th, and parked Maria's Pinto there. The last
known address for Charles S. Carruthers—according to his parole
officer's report—was 8212 McKenzie, four blocks west of Liberty, near the corner of 106th. The day was sunny and mild, and
the residents of Hammerlock were out in force to enjoy the good
weather, anticipating the winter perhaps, when they would be
imprisoned indoors in badly heated apartments. It was no accident that Hammerlock had the highest fire-incidence rate in
the entire city, or that most of those fires took place in the win-
tertime, when cheap and faulty kerosene burners were used to
supplement the heat that was *supposed* to be coming up in the
radiators; go fight City Hall.

The citizens regarded me with suspicion, partially because I was a white man in an exclusively black neighborhood, but more specifically because they knew I was fuzz. To them, it didn't matter that I was retired fuzz. Fuzz is fuzz, and there's a fuzz look and a fuzz smell. They knew *exactly* what I was, and they could guess at why I was there—to get one of their people in trouble. They were wrong. I was there looking for a white woman who maybe knew why a white man had stolen a corpse from a mortuary after killing a white employee of the place. But they were right, too. Fuzz *is* fuzz.

I know too many cops, especially detectives, who are very quick to assume a man is guilty of something or other simply because he looks "bad." Nine times out of ten, this means he looks "black," a condition over which he has very little actual control. I know a two-hundred-pound white detective, for example, who beat up a hundred-and-ten-pound black postal clerk coming home from work at two in the morning—because he looked "bad." He later charged the man with loitering and resisting arrest. I know another white detective—a pair of them, in fact, working as partners—who were investigating a narcotics case and busted into an apartment where a teenage black kid was puffing on a joint. That's all the kid had on him, that single joint, and it was almost down to a roach when they broke in. Otherwise he was clean. But their stoolie had told them there was a dope factory up in Apartment 6A, and this was Apartment 6A, and there was only a skinny black kid sitting on the bed in his undershirt, half stoned out of his mind on grass, and not knowing what they were talking about. They figured he looked "bad." They dropped three nickel bags of heroin on the floor, and they called in the cop on the beat to witness the arrest, and when the three cops testified against the kid in court, they made him sound like the dope king of the Western world. He's now doing time at Brandenheim, upstate. He probably will *still* look "bad" when he gets out.

Some black detectives aren't much better where it concerns

their brothers. Or sisters, as the case may be. I know a black Vice Squad detective who arrested a black woman for violation of Section 887 of the Code of Criminal Procedure—the section defining prostitution. In court, he claimed she came up to him on the street, asked if he wanted to have a good time, set a price, took him up to a hot-bed apartment, and "exposed her privates" to him, which in this city is the moment of truth before which no vice arrest can be made. The charge stuck. The woman was sentenced to a year's imprisonment at the state reformatory for women in Ashley Hills. No pimp came forward to put up bail for her while she was awaiting trial, no shyster lawyer got her off with a pat on the behind and a fifty-dollar fine. That's because she wasn't a prostitute, you see. She was a manicurist at a beauty parlor. The detective who arrested her had been stopping by the place for months, trying to make time with her. He'd finally got the courage to ask her for a date, and when she refused—she was a married woman—he busted her the next day.

I'm not trying to suggest that every cop in this city is bigoted or ignorant or merely short-sighted—the hell with that. I'm merely trying to explain why I was watched warily and silently and suspiciously and angrily as I walked past tenement stoops and markets, bars and billiard parlors, storefront churches, barbershops, banks, and empty lots—yes, even pre-school kids playing on heaps of rubble turned to look at me with undisguised hostility. Fuzz is fuzz.

The tenement in which Charles Carruthers lived was made of red brick, but it looked gray, just like all the others on the block. A fat woman wearing a blue dress and a dark-blue cardigan sweater was standing on the wide top step of the front stoop, holding a sleeping baby in her arms. I nodded to her and went into the entrance foyer. The mailboxes were just inside the door. A naked light bulb hung overhead. The locks on four of the boxes were broken. I could find no nameplate for Charles Carruthers. I went outside again.

"Excuse me," I said to the woman.

"Baby's sleepin'," she said.

"Do you know what apartment Charles Carruthers is in?"

"Nope," she said.

"I'm an insurance adjuster," I said. "I've been authorized by Allstate to turn over a check to Mr. Carruthers, but . . ."

"*Shit,* you're an insurance adjuster," the woman said. "You're a *cop* is what you are."

"I *used* to be a cop, you're right," I said. "How'd you know that?"

"Huh?" she said.

I reached into my pocket and took out the little black-leather case, and opened it, and showed her the gold shield, and said, "See where it says 'Retired'? Right there under the 'Detective-Lieutenant'?"

She looked at the shield and nodded. "Mm," she said.

"How'd you know I used to be a cop?" I asked.

"Jus' lucky, I guess," she said dryly, and studied me with a fresh eye, her head cocked to one side, the baby's head resting on the opposite shoulder. "You're an insurance man, huh?"

"That's right," I said.

"With Allstate, huh?"

"'You're in good hands with Allstate,'" I said, and smiled.

"And you got a check for Charlie, huh?"

"If I can find him," I said.

"Why'n't you just mail it to him?" she said.

"I need his signature. On the release form."

"How much is the check for?" she asked.

"Not much. Seventy-four dollars and twelve cents. But I'd like to close the file on this, and unless I can find him . . . *Does* he live in this building?"

"Upstairs," she said. "The fourth floor. Tell him when he cashes that check, he ain' to forget he owes me six dollars. Gloria, tell him. He'll know who you mean."

"Thank you," I said. "The fourth floor, right?"

"Tha's right. Apartment 42. Now don't you forget t'tell him, hear?"

"I'll tell him."

"Six dollars," she said.

I went into the building again. The glass panel on the upper half of the inner lobby door had been broken out completely; a gaping open rectangle revealed the stairway inside, garbage cans stacked to the left of it. I opened the door and climbed the steps to the fourth floor. There was the stench of contained living in the hallways, cooking smells and garbage smells and the smells of human waste. I listened outside the door to Apartment 42, and then knocked. A man's voice answered immediately.

"Yeah?"

"Mr. Carruthers?"

"Yeah?"

"Police officer," I said.

"Again?" he said. I heard him coming toward the door. It was apparently unlocked, I heard no tumblers being turned. He opened the door and looked out at me. He did not ask for identification, and I offered none.

"Come in, come in," he said wearily.

The description Dave Horowitz had read from Carruthers' yellow sheet had done little to suggest the handsomeness of the man. Carruthers was tall and muscularly built, his hair barbered in a modified Afro cut, his dark eyes alert and intelligent, his complexion a warm brown color. He was clean-shaven, dressed in form-fitting, bell-bottomed slacks and a long-sleeved white sports shirt with patch pockets, sandals on his feet. He had very big hands, with the outsized knuckles of a street fighter. A gold ring was on the index finger of his right hand.

"I already gave at the office," he said, and smiled.

"I take it my partner was here," I said.

"Man named O'Neil?"

"That's the one."

"He was here," Carruthers said. "You guys ought to try avoiding duplication. Save the city a little money." His smile was entirely charming. I found it difficult to remember he'd spent half of his life in prison.

"I hope you won't mind answering a few more questions," I said.

"Long as we make it fast," he said. "I got to get to work."

"What kind of work do you do, Mr. Carruthers?" I said. It was now four o'clock in the afternoon.

"I'm a dishwasher," he said. "I work at the R&M, up on Liberty. I go in at four-thirty, and I'm through by ten. It's a good deal."

"I guess you know why I'm here," I said.

"Natalie Fletcher," he said, and nodded. "Your partner finally got around to asking me about her, after an hour of bullshit. I guess I had to convince him first I didn't kill a man, and steal a dead body, and hit an old lady with a crowbar."

"I take it you convinced him."

"I convinced him because I was next door playing poker last night, and three guys in the game live right here in this building, and he talked to two of them, and they swore on a stack of Bibles that I was in Apartment 33 from eight-thirty to two in the morning. I also lost forty-seven dollars," he said, and smiled again.

"Did my partner mention why we're looking for Natalie Fletcher?"

"Your partner is a very close-mouthed person," Carruthers said. "He told me about the homicide only because he figured to scare hell out of me. He had me doing life at Brandenheim even before he walked through that door. But this time I'm clean. As clean as a field of daisies. Sit down. You want some coffee or something?"

"Thanks, no, I realize you're in a hurry. Mr. Carruthers, according to your parole officer . . ."

"Mr. Elston, yeah."

"According to him, you're living with Natalie Fletcher."

"*Was,*" Carruthers said.

"She's not living here now?"

"No."

"When *was* she living here?"

"She moved out three months ago. Took a pad on Oberlin Crescent."

"Mr. Elston seems to think . . ."

"Mr. Elston is a very nice guy, but he's also very old-fashioned. He thinks if you're living with some chick, that's it forever. Till death do us part, you know? He keeps asking me 'How's Natalie?' when I already told him maybe a hundred times I kicked her out."

"And that was three months ago?"

"June the eighth, to be exact. A Saturday. We had a very nice scene here. I'll never forget that night as long as I live."

"What happened?"

"What happened is Nat's crazy, that's what happened. And also, she almost got me in trouble. I went to one of her fuckin' witches' Sabbaths, and some guy tipped off Elston, and he started warning me about breakin' parole, and like that. Look, I'm leveling with you, mister, I don't want you going back to Elston and telling him I *did* go to that thing. I told him he was making a mistake, and he believed me. Anyway, I didn't go to any *more* of them. Crazy damn bitch," he said, and shook his head. "Everybody standin' around with black hoods over their faces, and doing the whole voodoo bit, and carvin' up chickens . . ."

"Chickens?"

"For blood sacrifices. A bunch of bullshit is what it was. If I'd known she was hipped on that devil shit, I never would've started up with her."

"How'd you meet her?"

"At a party downtown. I was the token spade, she was the obligatory kook. We hit it off right away. This was right after her brother died, I guess she was looking for somebody she could talk to. My *own* brother died when I was just a kid, so I knew how it felt. Also, she's a terrific-looking girl, I guess you know that. Or at least she *was* till she started coming on like Cleopatra, dyeing her hair black and starting to wear that shit around her eyes. Jesus!"

"When was that?"

"A little while after we began living together. Must've been the end of April, the beginning of May. I figured it was just some more of her kookiness coming out, you know? I mean, to tell the truth, it was the *kookiness* that attracted me to her in the first place. I'd had white ass before, even chicks who were better-looking than Nat, but none of them had that kookiness about them, you know? I never knew what to expect from her. It was like every day was some kind of surprise." He grinned suddenly. "When you're trying to make it straight, there ain't much excitement around, you know? You've got to be careful you don't spit on the sidewalk, otherwise you're back inside. Well, living with Nat made things exciting."

"Then why'd you kick her out?"

"Because there's a difference between a kook and a crazy. The minute I realized Nat was a crazy, I asked her to leave."

"Crazy how?"

"The brother thing."

"What about it?"

"Well . . . her mother gave Nat all this junk when her brother died. His personal stuff, you know? All kinds of shit—his birth certificate, some of his toys from when he was a kid, his Army discharge papers, his report cards from elementary school, his driver's license, his social security card, compositions he'd written in high school, his class ring from when he graduated college . . . a whole pile of worthless shit. But Nat used to take it out and go through it again and again, as if it was some kind of national treasure. And you know this pendant she wears all the time? This little jade thing with the carving of Cleopatra on it?"

"Yes, what about it?"

"It was a gift from her brother, I guess you know that."

"Yes."

"Okay. He gave it to her, I don't know when, her twenty-first birthday, I don't know, he found the pendant in an antique shop and gave it to her as a present. Had it engraved with her name. A nice gift."

"Go on."

"Okay. Right after we began living together, she tells me the gift was from Ptolemy the Twelfth, who her brother Harry has suddenly become in her mind, right? And she takes it to a jeweler and has him engrave it with the date Cleopatra was born—69 B.C. And she starts remembering things about Harry—who's now Ptolemy, right?—and telling me they got married when she was seventeen, and telling me how much she loved him, and then . . . Ah, shit, she just got crazy, that's all."

"How?"

"She started calling *me* Ptolemy. She started saying *I* was her brother. And in a little while I realized she wasn't fucking Charlie Carruthers on that bed in there, she was really fucking Ptolemy the Twelfth, who was Harry Fletcher her goddamn dead brother. Mister, I don't like being a phantom fuck. I told her to get out."

"And she left."

"She made a fuss. But she left. This was on the eighth of June. She came back on the fourteenth to get her stuff, told me she'd found an apartment on Oberlin Crescent."

"Have you seen her since?"

"Once. She came up to Hammerlock last month to show off her new boy friend. Must've been looking for me all night, driving around from bar to bar. Finally caught up with me outside

Dimmy's on a Hun'-third. I was just coming out of the place, I see her sitting in this VW bus. She waves me over and introduces me to the guy behind the wheel. He's white, naturally, and blond. *Very* blond. Big head of blond hair, blond mustache, blond eyebrows. Leave it to Nat. A spade kicks her out, so she latches on to the blondest stud I ever saw in my life."

"What color was the bus?"

"Red. With a white top."

"What was the man's name?"

"Arthur Wylie."

"What does he do for a living?"

"I don't know. I know only one thing, and that's he isn't gonna last too long, not with that hang-up she's got about her dead brother. There were times I thought she'd commit suicide or something, just so she could get to good old Harry. It was spooky. I had enough of that voodoo shit when I was a kid and my grandmother used to tell me stories. Seven years old, and she used to sit me on her lap and scare me out of my wits. I'm glad my grandmother's dead, and I'm glad I got rid of Natalie, too. I began to breathe again the day I kicked her out. I hope I never see her again as long as I live. One fling with Cleopatra was more than enough, believe me."

"Was that the last time you saw her? When she came up here with Wylie?"

"Yeah. But I got a call one night, I guess it was from her. I answered the phone, and a woman said, 'I put a curse on you,' and hung up. It didn't sound like Nat, but who else could it have been?"

"Susanna Martin?"

"Maybe," Carruthers said, and shrugged.

"You know her?"

"I know her. She's another crazy, thinks she's some goddamn witch who was hanged."

"Would you know if Natalie was living with Wylie?"

127

"Down on Oberlin Crescent, you mean? I don't know."

"Did you mention any of this to my partner?"

"Any of what?"

"Wylie? The VW bus?"

"He didn't ask. I told him only what he wanted to know. I hope you won't take this personal, but I didn't like your partner so much."

"The witches' Sabbath you went to. Where was it held?"

"I don't know. Nat blindfolded me when I got in the car, and she blindfolded me again when we left the place. That was all part of the bullshit, you see."

"Can you describe the inside of the place for me?"

"It was the basement of a church."

"But you have no idea where it was."

"It took us about an hour to get there."

"From here?"

"Yes."

"Okay, Mr. Carruthers," I said. "Thanks a lot."

"Am I supposed to expect you guys again, or what?"

"I don't think so."

"Your partner advised me not to leave town."

"That's cop talk."

"Sure, but cop talk scares me when there's a homicide involved. You think Nat had something to do with it?"

"I don't know. We found her pendant at the scene."

"Then she's got something to do with it," Carruthers said flatly. "She never took that thing off. Never. She wore it when she was in the shower, she wore it when we were in bed, she wouldn't part with it for her life. It was from her *brother,* don't you see? Her dear dead Harry."

I was walking toward the door. Carruthers opened it for me. I extended my hand.

"Thanks again," I said.

He took my hand and shook it. "Tell your partner I'm clean, will you? I've spent enough time on the inside."

"I'll tell him."

He closed the door behind me. I waited a few minutes, and then pressed my ear to the wood. Inside the apartment, Charlie Carruthers was whistling.

22

THIS CITY is divided into eight different sections, each with a telephone directory of its own. I checked the books for all eight, and came up with a total of twenty-seven Arthur Wylies scattered north, south, east, and west. With a little luck, if I started a door-to-door search that very minute, I figured I could visit all twenty-seven of them by next Saint Swithin's Day. I decided to call the Motor Vehicle Bureau instead. There are four police clerks attached to a special unit at the MVB, and their job is to provide information to any police officer, uniformed or plainclothes, investigating a case involving a motor vehicle. The girl who answered the phone sounded nineteen, and made me feel a hundred and four. I identified myself as Detective-Lieutenant Benjamin Smoke.

"Yes, Lieutenant," she said, "would you mind letting me have your shield number, please?"

"83-074-26," I said.

"Yes, and what squad is that, Lieutenant?"

"The Nine-One," I said, giving her the number of the squad I'd commanded in the dear dead days.

"And the telephone number there?"

"Aldon 7-6140."

"Is this a registration search?" she asked.

"It is."

"Yes, sir?"

"Arthur Wylie, no middle initial, suspect vehicle a red-and-white Volkswagen bus."

"What year, sir?"

"I don't have one. I'm looking for the man's address."

"I'll have to get back to you on this, sir."

"This is a homicide case," I said.

"Ah, yes," she said, "aren't they all?"

"Victim's name is Peter Greer," I said, "employee of Haskins Mortuary on Sixth and Stilson. Check with Lower Homicide, if you like."

"One moment, sir," she said.

I waited one moment, and then another, and then deposited a dime when the operator told me my three minutes were up. I was beginning to believe the girl was actually checking with Homicide, and that she'd come back on the line to tell me I was a fraud. Instead, when she did come back, she said, "I've got that information for you, sir. We have a 1969 Volkswagen bus, red-and-white, registered to an Arthur J. Wylie at 574 Waverly Street. Did you want the registration number?"

"Yes, please."

"S22 dash 9438."

"Thank you," I said, and hung up. I looked at my watch. It was now twenty minutes past four. Waverly Street was crosstown and all the way uptown, approximately a half-hour's traveling time from where I'd parked Maria's Pinto. I hurried back to the garage, paid and tipped the attendant, and drove off with a rising sense of gloom.

23

THE WOMAN who answered the door was a good-looking brunette in her middle thirties. She was wearing dark slacks and a pale-green sweater, no make-up and no shoes. Through the wood, I had told her I was a police officer, and now she asked to see my shield. She glanced at it silently and then stepped back into the apartment. I followed her into the living room. It was inexpensively but tastefully furnished; someone had made a small budget go a long way. We sat in chairs facing each other.

"I'm looking for Arthur Wylie," I said.

"I'm Helene Wylie," she said. "His wife." Her eyes were very blue. She squinted at me across the width of the room, giving the impression that she was either near-sighted or in pain. Her hands were folded tightly in her lap. "He isn't here," she said. "I don't know where he is."

"Would he still be at work?"

"No."

"How do you know that?"

"I just know. Why are you looking for him? Has he done something?"

"Mrs. Wylie, *is* your husband employed?"

"He *was* employed. I don't know what he is now. He left the job in July."

"What job was that?"

"He worked for a travel agency."

"Where?"

"Shangri-La Travel," she said. "On Holman and Sixty-first."

"But you don't know where he's working now."

"I have no idea."

"Mrs. Wylie," I said, "are you and your husband living together?"

"No," she said. "We were separated in March."

"Where is he living now?"

"I don't know. His lawyer doesn't know, either. He moved out of his old apartment in July, and we haven't been able to locate him since."

"What's the last address you have for him?"

"You won't find him there."

"How do you know?"

"I've been there. A Puerto Rican family is living in his old apartment."

"Why'd you go there?"

"I was worried about him. I hadn't heard from him, and then I got a call from Leon—the owner of the agency, Leon Eisner—and he told me Arthur hadn't shown up for work, so I . . . I went to his apartment. I thought he might be sick. He was living alone, you see, and I thought he might be sick. I went to find out. I love him, you see. I still love him."

"When was this, Mrs. Wylie? When did you go to his apartment?"

"In July, just after the holiday. The Fourth fell on a Thursday, and Leon called me on Friday to say Arthur hadn't come back to work. I went right over to the apartment."

"And he was gone?"

"Yes. Diaz. That . . . that was the name of the family living there."

"And you don't know where he is now?"

"No. I wish I did. I'm sure if we could talk this over, we could . . ." She shrugged, and then suddenly turned her head away and covered her face with her hand. I waited. She stood up, walked to where her handbag was resting on top of the television set, unclasped it, and took out a handkerchief. "I'm sorry," she said.

"Mrs. Wylie, why did you and your husband separate?"

"I honestly don't know."

"Was there another woman involved?"

"No. No, there wasn't. No."

"Are you sure of that?"

"Yes, I am. I asked him, you see. When he told me he . . . he wanted to leave, I . . . I naturally asked him if there was another woman, and he said, 'No, Helene, there's no one else, I simply want out.'" She blew her nose, and then sniffed. Her eyes were still wet. "After twenty years of marriage," she said, "he simply wanted out."

"Do you have any children?"

"No."

"Where does the marriage stand now?"

"I don't know. Arthur wants a divorce, and my lawyers keep telling me there's no holding a man who wants to go." She turned away again, fighting a fresh wave of tears. "Forgive me," she said. "It's just . . . if we had a little time, I'm sure Arthur and I could . . . could talk it over and . . . work it out, you see." She turned back to me. "I tried to explain that to him on the phone, the last time I spoke to him. Just before he disappeared."

"And what did he say?"

"He said he wanted the divorce. He said he was through negotiating. He said if I didn't agree to a settlement soon, I'd be sorry."

"*Had* you been negotiating for a settlement?"

"Yes, through our lawyers. I turned down every offer."

"Why?"

"Because I don't *want* a divorce. I knew the offers were fair, I know what his earning capacity is. He's held a lot of different jobs over the years, but his income hasn't varied that much. So I know he was making fair offers, even generous offers, I suppose. But, you see . . . if I agreed to a settlement, the next step would be a divorce. And . . . I don't want one. I want Arthur back."

"What kind of jobs has he held, Mrs. Wylie?"

"Oh, everything, you name it. He's a very ambitious person, he changed jobs whenever he got bored, or restless, or realized he was in a dead end. He has that marvelous quality of being able to find work anywhere. After the Korean War, when he got out of the Navy, he immediately got a job as a bank teller. This was in Seattle, we're originally from Seattle. Then, after we got married, we began working our way east, and Arthur found jobs in the most unlikely places. We'd land in a tiny little town on the edge of nowhere, and you wouldn't think there'd be work there for *anyone*, but the next day Arthur would come home, and he'd landed a job as a short-order cook, or an automobile salesman, or . . . well, *anything*, really. He sold storms and screens, he worked as a hairdresser, he sold real estate . . . He's a good provider."

"And this most recent job was with a travel agency."

"Yes. He took it because he expected we'd get a lot of free trips. He's always wanted to go to Europe, I think he expected Leon would send him over there to check out the various resorts, you know. But it was *Leon* who went every place. Arthur just sat in the office there and made hotel reservations and wrote out airline tickets . . . he was getting terribly bored. I'm not surprised he quit. Would you like to know something? I think Arthur felt he was getting no place in the job, and decided instead that our *marriage* was bad. Do you think that's possible?"

"Yes, it's possible," I said.

"I don't think he's coming back," she said suddenly. "I don't think I'll ever see him again."

"Why do you say that?"

"He hasn't sent me a dime since July, when he disappeared. Before that, he'd send me a check every month, a sum agreed upon by our lawyers. But there's been nothing since July. I think he's washed his hands of the entire matter."

"When he left here—when he left *this* apartment in March —what did he take with him?"

"His clothes, some books. That's all."

"His passport?"

"He didn't have a passport. He's never been outside this country."

"Any bankbooks? Stocks? Savings certificates? Bonds?"

"He left the bankbook with me. There's very little in it. We haven't been able to save much over the years."

"Have you made any attempt to locate him since July?"

"I called the Missing Persons Bureau. I thought of hiring a private detective, but I haven't got the money for that. My father's been sending me money, not very much, but enough to get by on."

"Mrs. Wylie," I said, "do you have any recent photographs of your husband?"

"Yes," she said, "I think so. Would you like to see them?"

"Please."

She rose and walked swiftly out of the room. She was gone for perhaps five minutes, during which time I heard her opening and closing drawers somewhere in the apartment. When she came back, she was carrying an album which she placed on the coffee table before me.

"Most of these are old," she said, "but there are some we took in February, just before he left."

I opened the album, skipped through the pictures of Helene and Arthur as teenagers, briefly scanned the pictures of him as a young sailor in uniform, and turned to the last several pages in the album.

"Those are the ones we took in February," Helene said. "We drove up to Maine for the weekend."

Most of the pictures were of Helene, but there were several

good shots of Arthur alone, and a few of both of them together, obviously taken by a third person. In all of her pictures, Helene was smiling. Arthur looked to be in his early forties, a sober-faced man with a pipe clenched between his teeth in every shot. His blond hair was bushy and high, rising from his scalp in a white man's Afro cut. His blond eyebrows were shaggy, his blond mustache was trimmed in a modified walrus style. All of the pictures were full-length shots, but photographs are some-times deceiving as to height and weight, especially when a man is wearing a heavy winter overcoat.

"How tall is your husband?" I asked.

"Five feet eleven," she said.

"How much does he weigh?"

"A hundred and ninety pounds. He's a big man. And very handsome."

I made no comment. Instead, I looked through the most recent pictures again. I had never seen Arthur J. Wylie in my life, but he looked vaguely familiar. Troubled, I turned back to the mid-dle of the album. There were photographs of the young marrieds at what appeared to be a ranch, more photographs of them against a backdrop of mountains, another of Helene leaning on the fender of a '64 Oldsmobile, one of Arthur holding a duck in his arms and grinning.

"When did he grow the mustache?" I asked.

"When he started working at the bank in Seattle. He thought it made him look older and more dignified."

"When was that?"

"Just after he got out of the Navy—1953, it must have been."

"Has he worn a mustache since?"

"Always. I wouldn't know him without it."

I kept flipping backward through the album, backward through time, until at last I came to the beginning, or at least the beginning of Helene and Arthur. There were pictures of Helene in a cheerleader's skirt and a white sweater with the letter S on it. There was a picture of Arthur behind the wheel of a '48 Chevy, his bushy blond hair partially hidden by a baseball cap tilted onto the back of his head. There were pictures of both of them in bathing suits, lying on a grassy slope beside a lake. There were pictures of Arthur in Navy uniform. One of these captured my attention because it had obviously been taken while he was still in boot camp. He had not yet grown the mustache, and his bushy hair was cut so close to his scalp that he looked almost bald.

I stared at the picture.

Then I closed the album, got to my feet, and said, "Thank you very much, Mrs. Wylie, you've been very helpful."

"What has Arthur done?" she asked. "You haven't told me what he's done."

Arthur J. Wylie had done two things for sure:

(1) He had "disappeared" to Oberlin Crescent in July, when—using the name Amos Wakefield—he'd rented the apartment across the hall from Natalie's.

(2) He had since shaved his scalp and his upper lip clean. No more bushy head of hair, no more walrus mustache. Only the shaggy blond eyebrows were there as reminders of "the blondest stud" Carruthers had ever seen in his life.

It always got down to love, money, or lunacy—Jesus, what a bore! How many times in the past had I investigated cases in which a man had left his wife, taken up with another woman, and then attempted a disappearing act? The fleeing husband always changed his name—did Arthur Wylie *have* to call upon the tired cliché of using his own initials, AW, when becoming Amos Wakefield? The runaway spouse also invariably disguised his appearance by bleaching his hair or dyeing it, growing a mustache or shaving one off, putting on glasses or tinted contact lenses, and taking a job totally unrelated to any job he'd previously held. In Wylie's case, the job would be no problem—he was a jack-of-all-trades and could presumably find work anywhere. And whereas an errant husband disappeared for a variety of self-styled reasons, the common denominators remained love or money; basically, he was weary of (a) any further emotional involvements with his former mate, or (b) continuing his financial obligations to her.

Classic. I was dealing with a classic husband on the run. As depressing as this realization was, it was followed within the next thirty seconds by an overwhelming sense of despair. It was then that I suddenly understood the entire scheme. And although I admitted it had taken at least a modicum of ingenuity to concoct, the stupidity of its execution disappointed me nonetheless. I now knew what would happen next. I didn't know *when* it would happen, or *where* it would happen, or even *how* Natalie and Arthur hoped to make it convincing after such sloppy foreplay, so to speak. But it would undoubtedly happen soon, unless I got to them first and stopped the urgent timetable that had been set in motion on Sunday night. The saddest part of it all was that it didn't even matter any more. Stop them or not, the damage had already been done; an innocent bystander named Peter Greer had already lost his life.

Despondently, I started the long drive downtown to Oberlin Crescent.

24

I DIDN'T EXPECT to find Wylie in his apartment, and he didn't disappoint me. Or, depending upon how you looked at it, his absence was grievously offending in that he was performing absolutely according to expectations. It was now close to six-thirty. Dusk was already upon the city, nighttime fast approaching; if Wylie planned to do with John Hiller's corpse what I anticipated he'd do, his scheme would best be implemented in the dark. Stan Durski looked puzzled. He had let me into the apartment with a passkey, and he followed me around now as I opened empty drawers and peered into empty closets.

"Looks like he flew the coop," he said.

"Looks that way. Did you see him go?"

"Nope," Durski said.

"Did he tell you he was moving out?"

"Nope. Makes no never-mind to me, though. Had the rent paid till October first. Only thing bothers me is all this furniture he left behind. Another load of crap to get rid of," he said, and shook his head.

"Mr. Durski," I said, "were you awake at eleven-thirty, twelve o'clock last night?"

"I was," he said.

"You didn't see Mr. Wakefield when he got home, did you?"

"Nope, I didn't."

I looked around the apartment again. I could find absolutely nothing that told me where he had gone. I thanked Durski, and then went downstairs and walked to the garage where Natalie Fletcher had habitually parked her station wagon. A different attendant was in the small office, but he was listening to the same rock-and-roll station. I identified myself, and told him I was looking for a 1969 Volkswagen bus.

"Red-and-white?" he asked.

"Yes."

"That's Mr. Wakefield's," he said. "He was in here just a little while ago. I almost didn't recognize the poor guy."

"What do you mean?"

"He had to shave off all his hair. His mustache, too. He's got some kind of skin disease, he told me. The doctor made him shave all his hair off. Something, huh? He looked like that guy on television. What's that guy's name, the one who plays the baldy-bean cop?"

"What time was he in here?"

The attendant looked at his watch. "About a half-hour ago," he said. "Put some valises in the bus, and drove off."

"Anything else in the bus?"

"Like what?"

"Like anything five feet eleven inches long?"

"Huh?"

"Anything wrapped up or covered?"

"No, I didn't notice anything like that," the attendant said.

"Were you here when he came in last night?"

"No, I go off at eleven. He must've come in after that. Manuel must've been here. He's got the eleven-to-eight shift."

"Have you got Manuel's phone number?"

"Huh?"

"I want to call him."

"Oh. Sure, it's on the wall there. You see that card there? That's all the guys who work here."

I looked at the card. There were half a dozen hand-lettered names on it. I found the name MANUEL HERRERA, and along-

side it his telephone number. "Thanks," I said, and went out into
the garage and dialed the number from the wall phone alongside
the men's room. The same stale urine stench assailed my nostrils.
A woman answered on the sixth ring. She spoke with a Spanish
accent. I told her I wanted to talk to Manuel, and she said,
"Wait a minute, please." I waited. When he came on the line, I
recognized his voice as belonging to the man who'd allowed me
to rummage through his trash basket the night before.

"This is Lieutenant Smoke," I said, "I talked to you last night
about Natalie Fletcher's Buick station wagon."

"Oh, yeah," he said. "How's it going?"

"Fine," I said. "Were you working when Amos Wakefield
brought his VW bus in?"

"Yeah," he said. "Came in close to midnight, must've been."

"Anything in the car?"

"What do you mean?"

"Did you happen to notice whether there was anything on the
floor of the car?"

"Just the rug," he said.

"What kind of a rug?"

"Just a rug he had rolled up."

"Did he say anything about it?"

"Just asked me to keep an eye on it, that's all. I parked it up
on the second floor and locked all the doors."

"Okay," I said. "Thanks a lot."

"Yeah, don't mention it," he said. He sounded puzzled. I hung
up and walked out of the garage. The sky to the west was shaded
from black to blue to purple where the last thin line of daylight
limned the tops of the buildings. I looked at my watch. It was
seven minutes past seven. It would be dark within the next five
minutes.

A rug. He had wrapped John Hiller's body in a rug. Had that
been Natalie Fletcher's idea? Had she remembered a time in her
youth when she'd been carried into Caesar's presence rolled in-

side a rug? I sighed heavily, found a pay phone that was *not* close to a toilet, called Henry Garavelli's shop, and got no answer. I then called my own apartment. I let the phone ring a dozen times, and then hung up. Lisette had already gone home.

25

IT WAS ten minutes to eight when I got to the Twelfth Precinct. The desk sergeant told me Captain Cupera was out. I asked for Detective Horowitz, and the sergeant told me *he* was out, too. I didn't bother asking for O'Neil. Instead, I politely inquired whether it would be okay to use the pay phone in the swing room. The sergeant shrugged. I walked away from the desk and into the next room. A patrolman was sitting there in his undershirt, drinking coffee. I had the feeling he was the same patrolman who'd been there yesterday. I went into the phone booth, closed the door, and dialed the Twelfth Precinct. In the muster room outside, I heard the telephone ringing.

"Twelfth Precinct," the desk sergeant said. "Sergeant Knowles."

"Captain Cupera," I said.

"Who's calling?"

"Deputy Inspector Walsh," I said.

"One moment, sir."

I waited.

"Captain Cupera," Coop said.

"Coop," I said, "this is Ben, don't hang up."

"Benny, I told you—"

"I'm right outside in the swing room," I said. "I've got some information for you."

"What kind of information?"

"I know who owns that Volkswagen bus, and I've got the registration number."

"Come in," he said. "I'm going to enjoy this."

I hung up and went out into the muster room again. Coop had already buzzed the sergeant. As I approached the desk, he said, "It's okay for you to go in. I wish they'd make up their damn minds." I crossed the room to the frosted-glass door and knocked.

"Yeah, yeah, come in," Coop said.

He did not offer me a chair. He pointed his finger at me instead, and said, "Don't ever say you're Walsh again, you hear me?"

"I'm sorry."

"Let me hear what you've got." An odd smile suddenly replaced his frown. A moment ago he had told me he was going to enjoy this. He was now beginning to enjoy it even before I began talking.

"The bus is registered to a man named Arthur J. Wylie at 574 Waverly Street," I said. "S22 dash 9438."

Coop was still smiling. He was making me very nervous. I realized he knew something I didn't know.

"Tell me," I said.

"Tell you what, Benny? I simply wish to commend you for your fine work. You're still a good cop, it's a shame you're not on the force."

"You already know who owns the bus, is that it?"

"We know."

"How long have you known?"

"Ever since the FBI got back to us."

"You found some latents on the crowbar," I said. "That's what was in the lab report."

"On the pendant," Coop said, and nodded. "A good thumb print. The I.S. came up negative, so we ran it through the FBI. They got back to us around five o'clock. Turns out the guy who left the thumb print was in the Navy during the Korean War. He didn't have a criminal record, but his prints were on file."

"Arthur J. Wylie," I said.

"That's who," Coop said.

"So the next thing you did was call the MVB."

"Very good," Coop said. "And they told us they had a red-and-white Volkswagen bus registered to an Arthur J. Wylie at 574 Waverly Street. We put out a teletype right away." He was grinning from ear to ear now; it was thoroughly obscene.

"And then O'Neil drove uptown to talk to Helene Wylie."

"That's exactly what he did," Coop said. "He wasn't too thrilled to hear you'd already been there. He must've missed you by maybe ten minutes."

"Did she tell him she hasn't been able to locate her husband since July?"

"She told him. Gave us a nice picture of him, too."

"Big blond guy, bushy hair, walrus mustache?"

"Yes."

"He doesn't look like that any more, Coop."

Coop seemed startled for a moment, but before he could say anything, the telephone on his desk rang. He picked up the receiver. "Captain Cupera," he said. "Yeah," he said. "Yeah. Where is it? Okay, right away." He hung up, immediately pressed a button in the base of the phone, and waited. "Danny," he said, "I just got a call from the Fifth downtown. They've found that VW bus." He listened for a moment, and then said, "All right, come on down. I'd like to go with you." He hung up and looked at me across the desk. "You heard," he said.

"I heard."

He lifted the receiver again, pressed another button in the base of the phone, and then said, "Sergeant, I'll be out with O'Neil. If Horowitz calls in, tell him we're down near the Tolliver Street Bridge, the approach road. He'll find it." He hung up, and looked at me again.

"Let me go with you, Coop," I said.

"We don't need you," he answered.

"There were times when you did," I said.

He didn't answer. But when O'Neil came downstairs, he told him I'd be following them to the scene. O'Neil frowned. He was wearing his hat on the back of his head, like a movie cop of the thirties. A day's beard stubble was on his chin and his cheeks. His mouth tightened.

"Why?" he asked Coop.

"He's been helpful," Coop said flatly. "I want him along."

The two men looked at each other.

"Just don't get in the way," O'Neil said to me, saving his dignity in the presence of his commanding officer. "This is a homicide we're investigating." He hitched up his pants, and I followed him and Coop outside.

26

THE TOLLIVER STREET BRIDGE spans two sections of
the city, crossing the Meredith River at its narrowest point
downtown. Warehouses line the streets in most of the surround-
ing area, and the neighborhood is deserted after dark. The
approach road to the bridge runs along the river's edge, on Avenue L. There is a metal guardrail separating the road from the
steep embankment dropping away to the river, but a twenty-five-
foot section of it was under repair, and it was precisely at this
spot that the Volkswagen bus had crashed through the erected
sawhorse barricades. It now lay smoldering on its side some fifty
feet below the road surface. Firemen were still dragging hoses
up the incline when we arrived. A pair of radio motor patrol
cars, their red dome lights flashing, were parked across either
end of Avenue L, sealing off the block. Another patrol car was
parked alongside one of the two fire engines. The driver of that
car was the man who'd radioed the accident report to the Fifth
Precinct. The desk sergeant there had recognized the license-
plate number as the one in Coop's teletype, and had immediately
phoned the Twelfth.

In the Police Department's *Homicides and Suspicious Deaths
Manual,* the investigating officer is advised to ask six questions of
the first officer at the scene. It is further suggested that he can
remember these six questions by utilizing the code word
NEOTWY, which is composed of the last letter in each of the
key words used to frame the questions. Anyone but an amnesiac

would remember the six key words, but in this city the Police Department takes no chances with its hired help. These six words are:

N – When

E – Where

O – Who

T – What

W – How

Y – Why

The investigating officer is told to use these words in their exact order. Detective Daniel O'Neil used them in their exact order now as he questioned the patrolman who'd called in the report. Coop and I stood beside him, listening. Everywhere around us, firemen were reeling in hoses and carrying equipment back to their engines. In the distance, I could hear the shriek of an ambulance siren.

"When did you discover the accident?" O'Neil asked.

"Must've been around seven-thirty," the patrolman said. "We just finished a circle of the warehouses, and was heading north up Avenue L when we spotted the fire down there. I called it in while Freddie, my partner, ran down the embankment with a fire extinguisher. It didn't help a damn, that thing was really blazing. Freddie come back up to the car, gave me the license-plate number, and I called that in, too. He was lucky. He was no sooner up here than the gas tank blew."

O'Neil skipped the "Where" question. He already knew where the VW bus was; it was fifty feet down the embankment. He went on to the "Who," phrasing his question somewhat differently than prescribed in the manual.

"Anybody in the bus?" he asked.

"There's a guy behind the steering wheel," the patrolman said. "Or what's left of him, anyway. I told the sergeant we were gonna need a meat wagon."

"You didn't touch him, did you?"

"No, *sir*," the patrolman said. He seemed offended that such a question had even been asked.

"Find anything on the street up here?" O'Neil asked. This was a variation of the "What" question. He was trying to determine exactly what had happened to cause the bus to crash through the wooden barricade.

"Like what, sir?" the patrolman asked.

"Skid marks, broken glass." Either of these might have indicated that a second vehicle had been involved in the accident; O'Neil was asking the right questions.

"I didn't see none, sir."

"Anyone witness the accident?"

"Not to my knowledge, sir. This area's pretty dead at night."

"Were there any vehicles on the street?"

"No, sir, not a single car. There's no parking allowed on the approach road, you know."

"I meant was there any moving traffic?"

"No, sir, the street was deserted."

"Okay, thanks," O'Neil said. He knew he wasn't going to get any valuable answers to the How or the Why suggested in the manual, and he didn't want to waste further time. Instead, he walked to where the car had gone off the road and through the barricade. Skid marks are usually visible to the naked eye, even on a surface that isn't wet or dusty, but there were no marks leading to the spot where the barricade had been breached. Nor were there any glass fragments on the road or on the muddy embankment beyond. Two of the sawhorses had been broken, apparently by the weight of the bus as it rolled over them; tire tracks in the mud showed the direction the bus had taken in its downward plunge. We were studying these tracks when we heard the ambulance approaching. The sound of the siren apparently reminded O'Neil that he'd need a medical examiner at the scene. He walked over to the patrol car and asked the driver to radio a request for one. He still didn't know who the victim of the accident was, but he knew he had a dead man on his hands. I didn't tell him that I already knew who was in that smoldering bus.

The interne and the ambulance attendants were annoyed at having to wait around till the M.E. arrived. O'Neil sent one of the patrolmen out for coffee, in an attempt to mollify them. It took forty minutes for the assistant M.E. to arrive. The fire engines were gone by then. He half slid, half ran down the muddy embankment to where the bus lay on its side. The front end had hit a huge boulder, and part of the roof and one door had been demolished in the resultant explosion. The subsequent fire had undoubtedly been intense; even the paint on the outside of the bus had been partially scorched away. The rear end of the bus was a total wreck, the metal torn open and twisted into sharp black tendrils of steel.

A man sat behind the steering wheel. The assistant M.E. turned away at the stench of burned flesh and hair. He tied a handkerchief around his face, covering his nose. A police photographer was busy taking pictures. His flash bulbs kept popping into the night, lending a curiously celebratory air to the macabre scene. When all the photos had been taken, the M.E. asked if it was all right to move the body out of the bus. O'Neil said it would be all right, and then asked the ambulance attendants and the interne to move it. They did so without comment, but it was plain to see they wished they were elsewhere. The M.E. put down his black satchel and got to work. O'Neil strolled over to me. We had been on the scene for an hour and a half already, but nobody yet knew who'd been incinerated inside that bus. Except me.

"What do you think?" O'Neil asked. His question surprised me. I hadn't expected him to ask me for an opinion.

"What do *you* think?" I said. I had been told by two cops I respected that O'Neil was a good cop. So far, he had done nothing to disabuse their opinions.

"It bothers me that there's no skid marks," he said. "There should be skid marks, don't you think? If the guy went off the road, there should be marks."

"Yes," I said.

"Also, did you notice those tracks in the mud? The car was pointed straight downhill. That's unusual, don't you think?"

"Yes," I said.

"I mean, if the guy lost control and went off the road, it's unlikely he would've gone through the barricade at that angle."

Coop walked over. "Danny," he said, "the M.E.'s got some stuff you'll want to tag."

"Thanks, Captain," O'Neil said, and walked back to the bus. Coop and I followed him.

The M.E. had found a scorched wallet in the dead man's pants pocket. The clothing covering his upper torso had been completely burned away, but tatters of fabric still clung to his legs. The M.E. handed the wallet to O'Neil, who immediately tagged it for identification and then went through it. The only things he found were twenty dollars in fives and singles and a browned but still partially legible driver's license. O'Neil read it, and then said, "Arthur J. Wylie."

"Let me see that," Coop said.

We looked at it together. The driver's license had been issued a year ago August, and would not expire for two years yet. The address on the license was 574 Waverly Street. The M.E. was removing a signet ring from the dead man's right hand. He told O'Neil which finger on which hand the ring had been taken from, and then handed it to him. The initials on the ring were AJW. O'Neil slipped it into an evidence envelope. From the dead man's left hand, the M.E. removed a wedding band. Again he identified the finger and the hand, and then passed the ring on to O'Neil. On the inside of the band the names *Arthur* and *Helene* were engraved, and immediately following them, the date *8/8/54*.

I looked down at the body. The face, the hands, and the front of the trunk had suffered the worst of the fire. Almost all of the head hair had been burned away, but several blond patches had escaped the inferno. The face was unrecognizable, a charred and shapeless mass of cooked meat. The burned and blackened fingers were hooked like claws. The stench was intolerable. A Police Department truck was inching its way down the embankment. The body was brightly illuminated for just a moment until the headlights turned away. Coop turned away, too.

"Jesus," he said.

"Fourth-degree burns," the M.E. said. "You can put that down as your cause of death."

The driver of the truck cut the engine. He came out of the cab and walked over to where they were standing. "Who's in charge?" he asked tonelessly.

"I am," O'Neil said.

"You want the bus lifted, huh?"

"Yeah."

"Okay, we'll get the winch on it," he said.

"I'm finished here," the M.E. said. "Let's tell the ambulance crew."

As we climbed the embankment, I fell in beside the medical examiner. He was a portly little man, and he was puffing hard against the grade.

"How are the teeth?" I said.

"The teeth?"

"The corpse's teeth. Did the fire damage them?"

"They're charred," he said, "but they're still in his head."

"Thanks," I said.

Below us, the men from the truck were shouting to each other as they attached their cable to the bus. When we got back to the road again, O'Neil was waiting for the M.E.

"What do you figure happened, Doc?" he asked.

The M.E. wasn't paid to make guesses, but he made one now. "Tank probably exploded on impact," he said. "The burns are typical. With explosions of this sort, the parts nearest to the blast are the ones that get most severely burned. In addition, he'd probably been cooking inside the bus for some time before the fire was extinguished. The dermis is contracted and brittle—did you notice those wide elliptic cracks? And the hair's all but gone, of course, cornea of the eyes opaque." The M.E. shrugged. "That's about it," he said.

O'Neil went over to tell the ambulance crew they could take the body. Some ten feet away, the police photographer was snapping pictures of the smashed sawhorses and the tire tracks in the mud. A reporter from the city's morning tabloid was on the scene. He asked Coop what had happened.

"No comment," Coop said.

"Hey, come on, Captain," the reporter complained.

"The area's restricted," Coop said. "I suggest you leave it."

The reporter put his hands on his hips and glared at Coop as he went down the embankment again. The winch had lifted the Volkswagen, and it was resting on all four wheels now. O'Neil had walked over to the motorized patrolmen who'd discovered the burning bus. Both of them were drinking coffee from cardboard containers. He was talking to the driver of the car when I approached.

". . . got on the scene," he said, "what'd the fire look like?"

"What do you mean?"

"Which part of the bus was burning?"

"The front end. You know where the driver's seat is? That's what was burning."

"And you ran down there with an extinguisher, huh?"

"My partner did. Freddie?" he said, and turned to him.

"Yeah," Freddie said. "I tried to squirt it through the windshield. The windshield was busted, and flames were leaping out of it, and all I could think of was the poor bastard behind the wheel. I guess I was trying to save him, you know what I mean? Though, prolly, he was already dead. Anyway, the extinguisher wasn't worth a shit against that kind of fire."

"Then what happened?" O'Neil asked.

"The extinguisher ran out, and I was afraid the tank might blow. So I took a quick look at the license plate and ran back up the hill."

"When *did* the tank explode?"

"Right after I got back to the car here. Ain't that right?" he asked his partner.

"Couldn't've been more than two or three minutes."

"Thanks," O'Neil said. As we started down the embankment again, he turned to me and said, "This stinks." He was right. It stank to high heaven. Coop was already down at the bus, going through the interior. He'd found the car's registration in the glove compartment, and he handed it to O'Neil now. The registration was made out to Arthur J. Wylie at 574 Waverly Street. The key was still in the ignition. There were several other keys on the chain. Two of them looked like house keys.

"I'll bet these fit the Waverly Street apartment," O'Neil said. He put the keys in an envelope, and then went into the rear section of the bus, where he found several charred remnants of what had once been a blue rug. The scraps were almost threadbare. One of them had a dark-brown stain on it.

"Blood?" Coop said.

"Maybe," O'Neil said. "The lab'll tell us." He tagged the scraps and put them in a large manila envelope. Then he turned to me and again said, "What do you think?"

"I think you're right about the absence of skid marks or broken glass," I said.

"Yeah," he said, and nodded. "There're a few other things that bother me, too."

"Like what?" Coop said.

"The burns. The M.E. said they were fourth-degree burns. On the face, the hands, and the front of the torso. Typical in an explosion. But the gas tank's in the *rear* of a Volkswagen bus. If the tank exploded *behind* Wylie, how'd he get the worst burns on the *front* of his body? Patrolman up there says only the front of the bus was on fire when he came down here with the extinguisher. The tank blew *after* he went back up the hill."

Coop was silent, thinking. I let them work it out together. I had no desire to step on O'Neil's toes. He was young, and not too experienced, but he was smart as hell, and he was covering all the bases.

"What's your guess?" Coop asked him.

"I think somebody doused the driver's seat *and* the driver with gasoline," O'Neil said. "Or some other volatile liquid, it doesn't matter. That bus was *pushed* over the embankment. When it hit the rocks down there, it exploded. Then the tank went up later."

"Benny?" Coop said.

"I think he's right."

"But you know what else bothers me?" O'Neil said. "If the guy wanted an explosion, how could he be *sure* he was going to get one? Even if he closed all the windows, how could he have known all that enclosed vapor would blow?"

"Maybe he just tossed a match in before he shoved the bus over," Coop said.

"Yeah, but that would've given him a *fire*, not an explosion. I've seen cars roll over a dozen times and not explode." He shook his head. "Well, however he did it, he damn well did it. This was no accident. Somebody *killed* Wylie." He was pleased with his deduction. So far, he had answers to the When, Where, Who, and What of NEOTWY. He was only partially sure of the How, but he was wondering about the same thing that bothered me:

How could the man have been *certain* he'd get an explosion? And, of course, he still didn't know Why. I decided to risk helping him.

"I don't think it was Wylie behind that wheel," I said.

Neither he nor Coop looked terribly surprised. The idea I'd expressed had not occurred to them before this moment, but they didn't grimace in derision, or exchange smiles or glances or winks. Even though the bus had been loaded with all sorts of identification, they knew the body had been incinerated beyond recognition, and so they waited for me to elaborate.

"Can you get Hiller's dental chart?" I said.

"Hiller?" Coop said.

"The corpse Wylie swiped last night," O'Neil explained. He was silent for a moment. Then he said, "Yeah, his dental chart. Yeah." He shook his head. "I've been going nuts trying to figure out why anyone would want to steal a dead body."

Coop was a little slower to follow the line of reasoning. When he caught on, he said, "Oh, *I* get it." His voice sounded almost childlike. "I'll be damned," he said, and he, too, shook his head.

O'Neil suddenly thought of something. "Jesus," he said, "the fire didn't *ruin* his teeth, did it?"

"No," I said. "The M.E. told me they're okay."

"Good," O'Neil said. He sounded enormously relieved. Teeth are as good as fingerprints when it comes to positive identification. All he had to do now was compare Hiller's dental chart with the teeth in the head of the incinerated corpse. That wouldn't tell him where the *real* Arthur Wylie was, but at least he'd then be certain his killer was still on the loose. "I want to get moving on this," he said. "Smoke," he said, and hesitated, and then awkwardly stuck out his hand. "Thanks."

He seemed very happy as we started the climb to the road. I did not tell him how depressed *I* was. There are some things employees of the Police Department simply do not understand.

27

IF I HAD FIGURED this correctly (and I was modestly certain I had), there was one thing Natalie and Arthur still had to do before leaving town forever. I knew *what* they had to do, and I knew *where* they planned to do it—but I didn't know *exactly* where. That's why I went back to the apartment.

I had put Henry on Natalie's tail at one-thirty this afternoon, and it was now close to ten-thirty and I'd heard nothing from him. The possibility existed, of course, that he had phoned the apartment sometime after Lisette left. The possibility also existed that he'd picked up Natalie's trail after her two o'clock appointment with Susanna Martin, and hadn't called for fear of losing her. There were other possibilities as well, and I considered these for a moment, never allowing hope to infringe upon reality—I knew the case was closed, I knew Arthur and Natalie were as good as in the bag. But suppose, ah, suppose?

Suppose Natalie *hadn't* kept her two o'clock date with Susanna? Or suppose Henry had picked up her trail as she left the building on Ninety-sixth, and then lost her later? Or suppose, even, that Natalie and Arthur did *not* plan to go where I expected them to go at midnight? Would this mean that they could ride over the horizon with obliterated pasts (*his* past, at least), free of Helene Wylie, free of police pursuit, free of anything but their own unlikely consciences?

Not a chance.

I knew who they planned to become, you see. Which was why

I was relatively certain they'd be at the midnight mass Natalie had noted on her calendar. The mass was to be held in their honor. The mass was to be a sanctification of sorts. Not legally binding, but Natalie had probably insisted on it, and if a man is willing to commit murder in order to escape his past, he's willing to go along with anything.

They'd had it.

Either tonight, or three weeks from tonight, or three months or three years, somebody would knock on their door wherever they were, and politely introduce himself as a cop, and just as politely inform them that they were being charged with the murder of one Peter Greer, not to mention the minor charge of having swiped John Hiller's corpse and set fire to it later. They would protest. I'm not Arthur Wylie, the man would say, you've made a dreadful mistake. Here, let me show you all sorts of identification, let me prove to you . . .

No, Arthur, it wouldn't wash.

Not tonight or any night in the future.

Just come along quietly, there's no death penalty for murder in this state.

Morosely, I sat in the kitchen and waited for the phone to ring. The apartment was unusually still; even the bird was silent. It occurred to me that I hadn't spoken to Maria all day, but I didn't dare phone her now and tie up the line.

"Are you hungry?" I asked the bird.

The bird said nothing.

"Edgar Allan?" I said. "Are you hungry?"

The bird peeped. He did not squawk, he did not yammer, he did not caw. He peeped. I went to the cabinet, took out a can of tuna fish, opened it, and spooned the contents into the cage. He was not a bad-looking bird. His black feathers were sleek and shiny, his eyes were intelligent and alert, and he certainly had a hearty appetite.

"That's a good bird," I said.

I did not know very much about birds, good or otherwise, but I seemed to recall (from the Hitchcock film I'd despised) that there was a difference between crows and blackbirds, and whereas Maria had offhandedly named *this* bird Edgar Allan Crow, wouldn't he take offense at such hasty baptism if he were *not* a crow but instead a black . . .

I suddenly remembered something.

"Excuse me," I said to the bird, and left him eating in his cage, and went through the apartment to my bedroom. I didn't bother looking through any of my dresser drawers. The only articles of clothing in the top drawer were handkerchiefs, underwear, and socks. My sweaters, in the middle drawer, were pullovers and cardigans, but they were in varying shades of blue (my favorite color) and wouldn't do. My shirts, in the bottom drawer, were white, blue, beige, and pink (just one, a gift from Maria). I opened my closet door. I owned a black sports jacket, but it had cost three hundred and fifty dollars to have it hand-tailored, and I certainly wasn't about to cut it apart, not for *this* miserable case. There was also a black raincoat hanging on the wooden clothesrod. I had bought it when I was in the Navy. The last time I'd worn it was in 1942, when I had "Peg" tattooed forever on my arm. I left the raincoat where it was, walked through the apartment again, and opened the door of the hall closet. "Raincoat" had triggered "rain," and "rain" had triggered "umbrella." Whereas my mother had always warned me never to open an umbrella in the house, I opened it now. It was black, all right, but was it big enough? I carried it into the kitchen, took a pair of scissors from the drawer near the sink, and got to work.

Occasionally, I glanced up at the clock. The phone refused to ring. It was eleven before I finished cutting the black silk. I carried the pieces into my study, placed them on the desk, and then went into the spare room Lisette used for ironing and for watching television, not necessarily in that order. From her sewing basket I took a needle, a spool of black thread, and a thimble. The last sewing I'd done was aboard the U.S.S. *Sykes* in the year 1946, just before I was sent home from the Pacific. This hardly qualified me as a tailor, though; I had fastened a button to a pea jacket and darned three pairs of socks. I sat down at the desk now, threaded the needle, slipped the thimble over my finger, and began hoping the phone would *not* ring till I was finished.

It rang at twenty minutes to midnight.

I snatched the receiver from the cradle.

"Hello?" I said.

"Ben, this is Henry."

"I've been waiting."

"I'm outside an abandoned church on Haley and Somers," he said. "The Fletcher girl is in there with a baldheaded guy. There's something going on."

"Give me ten minutes," I said.

"The truck's parked across the street, near a boarded-up Chinese laundry. If I'm gone by the time you get here, it means they took off, and I'll call you later."

"Right," I said, and hung up.

I took my holstered .38 Detective's Special from the bottom drawer of the desk, and clipped it to my belt. I did not know what to expect at the church on Haley and Somers, and whereas a rolling stone may gather no moss, a stitch in time most certainly saves nine. Gathering up my own stitchery, I stuffed the products of my handiwork into the pockets of my topcoat, and then left the apartment.

It was raining outside, and I'd just cut up my only damn umbrella!

28

‶How long have they been in there?”

"They went in maybe five minutes before I called you," Henry said. "I wanted to make sure they were staying before I looked for a phone booth."

We were sitting in the cab of his truck. The engine was running, and the windshield wipers swept aside the heavy rain, affording us a good view of the dark and silent church across the street.

"There's condemned signs all over it," Henry said, "and the windows are boarded up. I counted maybe two dozen people going in since Fletcher and the bald guy got here. They been going in one at a time or in pairs, Ben, through the back there—you see that gate in the iron railing?"

"Yes, I see it."

"A patrol car went by about ten minutes ago, but either they been paid to ignore it, or they didn't see nothing."

"Where'd you pick up Natalie?"

"Outside that building on Ninety-sixth, like you said. I followed her out to Hainesville. She went in a rooming house there, didn't come out again till almost dark. Then she drove down near the Tolliver Street Bridge—you know the bridge down there? Something must've happened down there, Ben. There were fire engines and police cars all over the place. Anyway, she picked up the bald guy about four blocks away from the bridge. He was carrying two heavy suitcases."

"Where'd they go after she picked him up?"

"They went to eat, and then to a movie. They came out about eleven-fifteen, and I followed them here."

"Good, Henry. You ready to go in there?"

"What's in there?" he asked.

"A wedding," I said.

He cut the engine, and we walked through the rain toward the church. An iron railing surrounded the small graveyard behind it. We went through the gate. As we approached an arched wooden door in the rear stone wall of the church, I reached into my pocket.

"Put this on," I said.

"What is it?"

"A hood. I hope the eyeholes are in the right place."

He took the hood and pulled it on over his head. "Very nice," he said.

"I made it myself."

"Very nice. I dig silk," he said.

I pulled the second hood over my own head, and then I knocked on the wooden door. We waited several moments. The door opened a crack.

"Yes?" a man's voice said.

"We're Cleopatra's guests," I said.

The door opened onto a small entryway constructed entirely of stone. The man who admitted us was short and squat. Like Henry and me, he was wearing a black hood over his head. He studied us through the eyeholes, and then silently indicated that we should go through the archway opposite the entrance door. There were iron hinges in the stone blocks supporting the arch, reminders of where another door once had been. We went through the archway and into a large vaulted room supported by stone pillars. The only illumination came from candles burning in sconces on the walls. An altar was at the front of the room, but if there had ever been pews, there was no evidence of them now. A large half-moon-shaped area of floor space had been left open before the altar, defined by the altar itself and the rough semicircle of folding chairs that had been arranged around it. On those chairs, at least three dozen black-hooded people were sitting. Henry and I found seats. I looked at my watch. It was five minutes to midnight. No one spoke. The windows in the room were boarded over from the outside, and the air was stale. More people came through the archway into the room. By midnight all of the seats had been filled, and several people were standing behind the circle of chairs.

To the left of the altar, black curtains parted. A hooded figure in a black robe moved swiftly to the altar. Even before she spoke, I knew from the erect carriage that this was Susanna Martin.

"Welcome," she said. "I welcome you in the name of Lucifer, and in the name of Beelzebub, his Prime Minister. I welcome you for Astorath, the Grand Duke, and for Lucifuge and Satanachia, Agaliarept and Fleuretty, Sargatanas, Nebiros, Agares and Marbas, Bathim and Bael, Nuberus and Aamon, and all others in the infernal hierarchy. I bid you welcome for them, and I bid you, also, to reaffirm now the Satanic Oath we each have separately and in the presence of this company sworn before."

She raised her arms like a stickup victim, bent at the elbows, the wide black sleeves of the robe falling back to reveal pale white flesh, the palms of her hands turned to the semicircle of silent, hooded people.

"We, Lucifer," she said, "and all beforementioned and following spirits . . ."

"We, Lucifer," they repeated, "and all beforementioned and following spirits . . ."

"Swear to you, to almighty God through Jesus of Nazareth . . ."

"Swear to you, to almighty God through Jesus of Nazareth . . ."

"The Crucified One, our conqueror . . ."

"The Crucified One, our conqueror . . ."

"That we will faithfully perform everything written in the Liber Spiritum . . ."

"That we will faithfully perform everything written in the Liber Spiritum . . ."

"And never do you harm, either to your body or your soul . . ."

"And never do you harm, either to your body or your soul . . ."

"And execute all things immediately and without refusing . . ."

"And execute all things immediately and without refusing."

The room went utterly still.

"I will summon Satan to this company," Susanna said.

Henry turned his hooded head to look at me. At the altar, Susanna bent out of sight for a moment. When she stood again, she was holding in her hands a long black box, shaped somewhat like a child's coffin. She carried this around the altar, holding it by the ornate silver handles on either end, and then stepped down onto the open floor space circumscribed by the folding chairs. She knelt swiftly and gracefully, put the box down on the floor and, still kneeling, lifted its lid. From the box she took a pair of silver candlesticks, and fitted black candles into them. She carried these to the center of the floor, lighted both candles, rose, and walked quickly back to the box. When she returned again to the burning candles, she was holding a long twig in one hand and what appeared to be a quartz crystal in the other.

"This is a bough of hazel," she intoned.

"Cut last night," the hooded figures responded.

"With a new knife," she said.

"From a tree that has never borne fruit," they said.

"As prescribed in the Great Grimoire, the book of medieval magic."

"Summon the Devil," they chanted.

"And this is a bloodstone, as further prescribed."

"Summon the Devil," they chanted.

Using the bloodstone, Susanna traced an invisible triangle around the candles on the floor, and then a large circle that encompassed candles and triangle. She stepped into the triangle and knelt to place the bloodstone between both silver candlesticks. Then, standing fully erect again, she grasped the hazel wand in both hands, left hand clutching one end of it, right hand clutching the other.

"I will repeat the Grimoire invocation twice, summoning Lucifer, Lord of the Infernal Hierarchy."

"Lucifer, our Lord," they chanted.

"I conjure you, Great Spirit," she said, "to appear within a minute, by the power of Great Adonai, by Eloim, by Ariel and Johavam, Agla and Tagla, Mathon, Oarios . . ."

The recitation seemed endless. In order to reach Lucifer, one apparently had to call upon a battery of lesser demons. "Almouzin," she said now, "and Mebrot," standing in the center of her invisible triangle, "Varvis, Rabost," the candles flickering at her feet, which I noticed were bare, "Salamandrae, Tabost," both hands clutching the hazel wand, "Janua, Etituamus, Zariatnctmik."

Her voice stopped abruptly. Scarcely pausing to catch her breath, she went through the ritual a second time, just as she had promised, and this time I began counting. Before she stopped again, I'd counted twenty-seven names in all.

She dropped to her knees. There was the sudden sound of chair legs scraping against the stone floor as the black-hooded assemblage, following her lead, knelt in worship to whomever she had conjured. I saw no one. Neither Lucifer nor any of his demons were visible to my eyes, but Susanna's body stiffened, and she touched her forehead to the floor and placed her trembling hands palms-down on the stones. A single word hissed sibilantly from beneath the black hood.

"Master."

"Master," they whispered.

What followed was the equivalent of eavesdropping on someone making a long-distance telephone call—a *very* long distance,
in this case. I could hear Susanna's voice, of course, but I could
not hear Lucifer responding. I had dropped to my knees the
moment the assemblage had. Henry was kneeling beside me. His
arm brushed mine; he was shaking.

"We are honored," Susanna said.

(Silence)

"We summon you tonight to witness and to bless the union of
a pair devoted to you and to each other."

(Silence)

"We beg that you observe, and pray we do not suffer your
wrath for grievous omission or inadvertent error. May I rise?"

(Silence)

She got to her feet.

"May we rise?" the assemblage asked.

(Silence)

They rose, the semicircle of black hoods floating upward like
malevolent balloons. A pair of similarly hooded figures parted
the curtains and walked hand-in-hand past the altar. They
stepped down to the open floor space and knelt before the burning black candles. Susanna held out both hands and rested them
on the bowed heads of the couple.

"Master," she said, "we beseech you to receive this woman,
known to you in ancient times as Cleopatra, daughter of the Nile,
Queen of all Egypt, proud possessor of the Ptolemaic name."

"We beseech you to receive," the assemblage chanted.

"We beseech you, too, to receive her in her present form, as
Natalie Fletcher, who is here this midnight to wed anew but to
wed again, we beseech you to receive."

"We beseech you to receive," they chanted.

"We beseech you to receive as well her intended groom, who

casts aside the hated name bestowed in keeping with the Christian belief, through baptism vile, in ceremony honoring Jesus of Nazareth, the Crucified One, our conqueror, we beseech you to condemn to blackest night the name of Arthur Joseph Wylie . . ."

"We beseech you to receive, we beseech you to condemn . . ."

"And accept as supplicant the reborn Harry Fletcher, brother to Natalie, and by profound belief, the brother, too, of Cleopatra. We beseech you to receive Ptolemy the Twelfth, who by virtue of this solemn ceremony forswears allegiance to all other masters, renounces and forsakes the Jesus who renounced you, and swears that he will faithfully perform everything written in the Liber Spiritum, and never do you harm, either to your body or your soul, and execute all things immediately and without refusing. We beseech you to receive."

"We beseech you to receive."

Susanna looked down at the kneeling couple. "Do either of you know of any reason why you both should not be joined in wedlock, or if there be any in this company who can show any just cause why these parties should not be joined, let him now speak or hereafter hold his peace."

The vaulted room was silent.

Susanna knelt, picked up the bloodstone from where it was resting between the burning black candles, rose again, and touched the stone to the hooded forehead of the figure on her left.

"Do you, Harry Fletcher, take this woman as your wife to live together in the state of matrimony? Will you love, honor and keep her as a faithful man is bound to do, in health, sickness, prosperity and adversity, and forsaking all others keep you alone unto her as long as you both shall live?"

"I do."

Susanna moved the bloodstone to the hooded forehead of the figure on her right.

"Do you, Natalie Fletcher, take this man as your husband to live together in the state of matrimony? Will you love, honor and cherish him as a faithful woman is bound to do, in health, sickness, prosperity and adversity, and forsaking all others keep you alone unto him as long as you both shall live?"

"I do."

"For as you both have consented in wedlock, and have acknowledged it before this company, I do by virtue of the power invested in me now pronounce you man and wife in the presence of our Lord and Master. And may He bless your union."

She held out the bloodstone. They each kissed it in turn, raising the hoods briefly, and then lowering them over their faces again. I nudged Henry. I thought the ceremony was over, and I wanted to catch Natalie and Arthur before they ran off on their honeymoon. But they continued to kneel before Susanna, who now spread her arms wide, holding them above her head in an open V. Apparently, there was more business to conduct.

The curtains parted again. A tall hooded figure came through them and walked swiftly to where Susanna was standing. In one hand he was carrying something with a black cloth over it. In the other hand he was carrying a carving knife. He knelt before Susanna, waiting.

"We beseech you, ancient serpent," she said, "to accept this sacrifice of blood as token of this solemn union." She nodded. The black cloth was pulled away, revealing a cage. Something squealed. A hand darted into the cage, there was another squeal, the knife flashed out, there was silence.

"We beseech you now . . ." Susanna said.

"We beseech you now . . ." the assemblage repeated.

"We beseech you, judge of the living dead who orders the winds and the sea and the tempests, we beseech you . . ."

"We beseech you . . ."

"Master of the Lower Regions, to leave us now in peace,

knowing we are pleased and contented, and to go in quiet, secure in our faith. We beseech you."

"We beseech you," they whispered, and the room fell silent again.

Susanna suddenly laughed and clutched Natalie to her in embrace. The ceremony was over and done with, Lucifer had apparently gone back to Hell in peace, secure in the knowledge of their faith, stinking of brimstone, trailing silken garments, and pouring lower-case smoke from his pointed hairy ears. The assembled worshippers were moving toward where the black candles now sputtered fitfully in the silver candlesticks. There were cries of congratulation, and more embraces.

"Let's go," I said to Henry.

We moved swiftly to the archway at the back of the room, and then through it to the thick wooden entrance door. It was still raining outside. We took off the hoods.

"Where'd she park the station wagon?" I asked.

"Up the street," Henry said. His eyes were wet.

"Are you all right?"

"Weddings make me cry," he said.

They came out of the church not five minutes later. They had taken off their hoods, and they walked rapidly toward the blue Buick. They were chattering gaily. As Natalie unlocked the car, Arthur said something that made her laugh. Henry and I moved out of the doorway across the street, and ran to the car.

"Mr. and Mrs. Fletcher?" I said.

Natalie turned. She was extraordinarily beautiful, long black hair wet with rain, brown eyes accentuated by black mascara and green shadow, generous mouth tinted blood-red. She must have assumed Henry and I were well-wishers, guests who'd taken off our hoods and followed them outside to offer our congratulations. She was smiling. Her eyes were bright. Her face looked almost radiant. Beside her, Arthur Wylie frowned. He had recognized me at once, from our early-morning meeting the night before, when he'd told me he was Amos Wakefield. He grabbed her arm. He was ready to bolt. And then he saw the gun in my hand.

"I think you'd better come with me," I said.

29

WE DROVE to the Twelfth Precinct in Maria's Pinto, Henry at the wheel, Natalie sitting beside him, Arthur and I on the back seat. I did not holster the gun. When we got uptown, Henry said he preferred waiting outside in the car; police stations made him nervous. The newlyweds walked up the broad flat steps ahead of me. I put the gun away only when we were standing before the muster desk. The sergeant rang the squadroom upstairs, and O'Neil and Horowitz both came down. They were surprised when I told them the baldheaded man standing beside me was Arthur Wylie; the picture they had was of a bushy-headed blond with a walrus mustache. They booked Natalie and Arthur, advised them of their rights, and then called the district attorney's office. I was not permitted to be present at the Q and A. The assistant D.A. felt this might jeopardize their case, and I agreed with him. But when it was all over, at 2:30 A.M., they allowed me to read the transcript. Natalie had refused to say a word; she considered this her royal privilege. It was Arthur Wylie who did all the talking.

Q: What is your name, please?
A: Arthur Joseph Wylie.
Q: Where do you live?
A: I have no permanent residence in this city. Until tonight, I was living at 420 Oberlin Crescent.

Q: Mr. Wylie, would you please look at these items we took from your wallet? Do you recognize them?

A: Yes.

Q: Would you identify them, please?

A: That's a driver's license, and that's a social security card.

Q: To whom were the license and the social security card issued? Would you please read the name on them?

A: They were issued to Harry Fletcher.

Q: Can you tell us who Harry Fletcher is or was?

A: He was Natalie Fletcher's brother. He died six months ago. Of a heart attack.

Q: But you're carrying *his* identification in your wallet, is that correct?

A: Yes. Natalie's mother gave her all his stuff when he died.

Q: Why are you carrying his identification, Mr. Wylie?

A: That was the plan.

Q: What plan?

A: To become Harry.

Q: Why did you want to become Harry?

A: I had to. My wife refused to divorce me.

Q: What is your wife's name?

A: Helene Wylie.

Q: Are you separated from her at present?

A: We've been separated since March.

Q: When did you decide to become Harry Fletcher?

A: After I met Natalie.

Q: When was that?

A: When I moved to Oberlin Crescent. In July. I took the apartment at the beginning of July, and I moved in on the Fourth.

Q: And that's when you met Natalie?

A: Yes.

Q: Have you been living with her since July?

A: Yes. Well, we still kept the two apartments, but yes, we were living together. You could say we were living together.

Q: And was it in July that you decided to become Harry Fletcher?

A: Sometime in July, yes. I'd already decided to run away, you see. When I took the apartment on Oberlin Crescent, I used the name Amos Wakefield. That was in case my wife put detectives on me. I didn't want her to find me. I knew I was going to disappear forever, but I didn't know how yet. I was just buying time till I could figure out a plan.

Q: When did you figure out your plan?

A: In July, like I told you. I was with Natalie and she began showing me all this stuff she had. Her brother's stuff. Everything I needed to become another person. Birth certificate, discharge papers, everything. That was when I hit on the plan.

Q: And what was the plan?

A: I told you. To *become* Harry Fletcher. But there were problems, there were still things to work out. Because even if I became another person, my wife would still be looking for me, wouldn't she? So I decided to prove to her that I was dead.

Q: How did you expect to do that?

A: By stealing a corpse and putting my identification on it, and mangling the body.

Q: Mangling it?

A: I thought of using acid at first. On the face and the fingertips, you know? But then I figured that would be too suspicious. I also thought of cutting off the head and the hands, but that didn't sound so good, either. So I decided to fake an explosion in my own car. That would make it look more plausible, you know? If they found me burned to death in my own car.

Q: Did you, in fact, steal a corpse for this purpose, Mr. Wylie?

A: Yes. Well, actually, I stole *two* corpses. But I got rid of the first one.

Q: When did you steal the first one?

A: Sunday night. I broke into five funeral parlors before I found the right body. Or at least what I *thought* was the right body. I'd have gone on all night till I found one.

Q: What specific body were you looking for?

A: Well, somebody about my height and build. And my color eyes. I didn't know what the fire would do to the eyes. So I had to have the right color eyes. The hair didn't matter. I bleached the hair on the body I put in the Volks, anyway; I did it with peroxide. But the eyes bothered me. And also, it had to be somebody about my age, too. I knew the explosion would do a good job, but I didn't want anybody saying Hey, this corpse is a little short guy, and Arthur Wylie was a tall person. Or this guy looks to be an old man, and everybody knows Arthur Wylie was only forty-three years old. So I had to be very careful what body I stole.

Q: Where did you steal the first body?

A: On Hennessy Street. I don't know the name of the place. I just had a whole list of funeral parlors, I made the list very carefully, it took me almost two weeks to make that list. And I planned to hit them one by one till I found what I wanted.

Q: And you found what you wanted?

A: I thought I did. Then I looked over the body, and I discovered somebody had cut it open above the belly, and under the arm, and near the, you know, the genitals, and also on the front of the neck. And I realized that must've been done when they were embalming it. I didn't know how close the body would be inspected after the fire, but suppose they saw those cuts, and also suppose they found formaldehyde inside the body—I didn't know whether the fire would take care of that. Suppose it didn't, and they realized they had an embalmed corpse there? How could I already be embalmed if I just got burned to death in a car accident? So I dumped off the first body and I went looking for another one the next night. Last night. Natalie was already gone by then.

Q: Where had she gone?

A: Well, to the new apartment.

Q: Where's the new apartment?

A: It's not an apartment, actually, it's a rented room. In Hainesville. We planned to stay there till we read the papers and knew everything had come off the way we figured. Then we were going to Europe. We planned on going to Europe in October. I've always wanted to go to Europe. I was going to use Harry Fletcher's birth certificate when I applied for a passport.

Q: Where did you steal the second body?

A: From a place on Sixth and Stilson.

Q: Was that the body of John Hiller?

A: I don't know who he was. He was my size and about my age. I went in there, and he was laying naked on the table, and he looked about right. I didn't know anyone was in the place. I was about to take the body when someone asked me what I was doing there. I turned around and . . . there was a man standing there, and I . . . I . . .

Q: Yes, Mr. Wylie?

A: I picked up a knife from the table. The table the body was on. And I . . . I guess I stabbed him.

Q: Would you look at this photograph, please? Is this the man you stabbed?

A: Yes.

Q: What did you do next?

A: I picked up the body . . . the one that was on the table . . .

Q: You picked up the body of John Hiller?

A: If that was his name.

Q: That was his name.

A: I picked him up and carried him outside. I was putting the body in the bus when a dog began barking, and I saw an old lady standing there looking at me. I guess I . . . I got very frightened then. I had just stabbed a man, and she was looking at me, and even though I planned to shave my head and my mustache, suppose she described Arthur Wylie to you, and later you find what's supposed to be Arthur Wylie burned to death, wouldn't you make a connection? I mean, wouldn't you know why Arthur Wylie had stolen a dead body? So I . . . I went after her, and I guess I would have killed her, too, but she started yelling and people were beginning to look out their windows, so I dropped the crowbar and got out of there fast.

Q: Mr. Wylie, do you recognize this pendant?

A: I do.

Q: Whose pendant is it?

A: It's Natalie's.

Q: Natalie Fletcher's?

A: Yes. It's hers.

Q: Were you wearing it when you stole the body of John Hiller from the mortuary at Sixth and Stilson?

A: I was. I must've lost it when I was struggling with the old lady. She was ripping at my clothes, she scratched my face, she was a terrible old lady.

Q: Why were you wearing Natalie's pendant?

A: She gave it to me for luck.

Q: When?

A: Sunday. Before I went out looking for a body.

Q: The night you stole the corpse from Abner Boone's mortuary?

A: I don't know the name of the place. The one on Hennessy Street. Where I got the embalmed body.

Q: And you were still wearing it last night, when you stole the second corpse?

A: Yes. Well, I still needed luck, you see.

Q: When did you shave off your mustache and the hair on your head?

A: After I got the second body. I wrapped it in an old rug Natalie used to have in her apartment, and I left it in the

VW bus when I parked it. I didn't want to risk carrying it any place, I figured it would be safe there till the next day. When I got back to the apartment, I put a Band-Aid on my face where the old lady had scratched me, and then I shaved off the mustache, and cut off my hair and shaved my scalp clean.

Q: What time did you leave the apartment on Oberlin Crescent tonight?

A: About six-thirty. I gave myself plenty of time. I knew where I was going to fake the explosion, and I knew it only took a half-hour to get there from my apartment. But I still had to get the gasoline. You see, I'd gone to a hardware store on Saturday, and bought a plastic five-gallon container, you know, with a cap on it and a pouring nozzle—cost me six dollars and fifty cents. But I still had to fill it with gas. So the first thing I did was find a gas station, and have them fill it for me. Then I drove around till it got dark, and when I got to the approach road, I had to wait another five minutes because some guy was parked there, reading a road map. When he left, I got the bus in position, took my valises out of it, and put the body behind the wheel. Then I poured the gas over the body and the front seat.

Q: How could you be sure the gasoline would explode?

A: Oh, I was sure.

Q: How? The engine and the gas tank are in the rear of a Volkswagen bus.

A: Oh, sure, I know that. But you see, what I did was push in the cigarette lighter just before I rolled the bus over the edge. It takes twenty-five seconds for the lighter to get hot, I timed it. I pushed in the lighter, got out of the bus fast, shoved it over, and then watched it go down the embankment. It exploded the second the lighter got hot.

Q: What did you do after the bus exploded?

A: I picked up my valises, and also the empty container, and I started walking toward where Natalie was going to pick me up. I dropped the container in a garbage bin outside one of the warehouses. Natalie was already there when I got to Avenue K and Ulster. By that time I could hear fire engines coming.

Q: And then?

A: We went out for a bite, and then we went to a movie.

Q: What movie did you see?

A: I'd seen it before, when it was first playing. But it's around again, and Natalie wanted to see it.

Q: What movie is that?

A: *Mary Poppins.*

I drove Henry downtown to where he'd left the truck. The rain had let up, but the sky was still overcast, and the night was very black. We had talked about the case on the way from the Twelfth, and now Henry said, "He shoulda just killed the wife. That was the easy way to do it."

"He hadn't planned on murdering anyone," I said. "That just came up."

"Well, you go around stealing dead bodies, you got to *expect* something to come up," Henry said, and yawned. He got out of the Pinto and extended his hand. "Ben," he said, "I'll see you."

I waited until he had started the truck, and then I drove off. I found an all-night diner three blocks away, got out of the car, and phoned Maria. She answered on the second ring.

"Ben?" she said. "Are you all right?"

"I'm fine, Maria," I said. "May I come there?"

"Of course," she said.

"I may be a little while. I want to go home first, check on Edgar Allan."

She hesitated. "Are you keeping him?" she asked.

"I've been thinking about it. He's not a bad person."

"Ben?" she said.

"Yes, Maria?"

She had heard the tone of my voice, she knew what I would answer even before she asked. "You solved it, didn't you?" she said.

"Yes," I said. "I solved it."

"You poor darling," she said.